# Praise for Ann Warner's Novels

## *Dreams for Stones*
### Indie Next Generation Book Awards Finalist

…incredibly vivid and emotional tale of love and loyalty, friendship, loss, and faith…*Booklist*

…a lovely story about life changes and love lost and found. *Romantic Times Book Review*

Stunning! Juli Townsend, Author of *Absent Children*

## *Absence of Grace*

…a riveting read of personal struggle, very much recommended. *The Midwest Book Review.*

Both a coming of age and a romance novel, this story is captivating and charming. But be prepared, you may not want to put it down once you start. Karen Bryant Doering, author of *Parents' Little Black Book*

…the writing is perfect. Absolutely smooth and divine. Like the best bar of chocolate. Fran Macilvey, author of *Trapped*

## *Counterpointe*
### Endorsed by Compulsion Reads

…a powerful novel of two lovers who face profound challenges. Poignant and insightful…a compelling dramatic evaluation of what it means to love or be loved. *The Midwest Book Review*

…a wonderful exploration of two people from different worlds coming together and finding love and building a lasting, realistic relationship with all the complexities, joys and sorrows that entails. *Long and Short of it Reviews*

Ann's brilliant, well-thought-out prose lifts her stories to a higher literary level than most of today's fare…prepare to be impressed. Pam Berehulke, Bulletproof Editing

## *Love and Other Acts of Courage*

*Love and Other Acts of Courage* is…beautiful. The plot is engaging and it focused on the development of the characters…and the ending (is) very satisfying. Lorena Sanqui for Readers' Favorite

…a love story woven within an engaging mystery with twists and turns, believable villains, and enough tension to keep you turning pages. Dete Meserve, author of *Good Sam*

…the characterizations of Max, Jake, and Sophie are done so delicately, so perfectly, that each alone would be worthy of a separate story. In short, Love and Other Acts of Courage is so much more than a love story. Kate Moretti, NY Times bestselling author of *Thought I Knew You*

## *Memory Lessons*

…you don't want to miss this inspirational story. David Johnson, author of *The Tucker Series*

…a real treat if you like to read novels that make you feel. Margaret Johnson, author of *The Goddess Workshop*

…high-stakes drama with real characters and an understanding of how women process memory and guilt. Patricia Macauliffe

A lovely and compelling story. Michelle Lam, author of *The Accidental Prophetes*

Look for these titles by
Ann Warner

*Absence of Grace*
*Counterpointe*
*Love and Other Acts of Courage*
*Doubtful*
*Memory Lessons*
*Vocabulary of Light*
*Dreams for Stones*
*Persistence of Dreams*
*Unexpected Dreams*
*The Babbling Brook Naked Poker Club Series*

# The Babbling Brook Naked Poker Club

## Book Four

by

# Ann Warner

The Babbling Brook Naked Poker Club - Book Four

Copyright © 2019 Ann Warner

Library of Congress Registration

TXu 2-174-106

Edited by

Pam Berehulke, Bulletproof Editing

Cover design by

Kit Foster Design

ISBN: 9781713225744

This e-book is licensed for your personal enjoyment only and may not be re-sold, but if you would like to share with a friend, this e-book is enabled for lending. Thank you for respecting the hard work of this author.

Without limiting the rights under the copyright reserved above, no part of this publication may be reproduced, stored in, or introduced into a retrieval system, or transmitted in any form, or by any means (electronic, mechanical, photocopying, recording, or otherwise) without the prior written permission of the above author of this book.

This is a work of fiction. Names, characters, places, brands, media, and incidents are either the product of the author's imagination or are used fictitiously. The author acknowledges the trademarked status and trademark owners of various products referenced in this work of fiction, which have been used without permission. The publication/use of these trademarks is not authorized, associated with, or sponsored by the trademark owners.

*Dedication*

To all my mentors.

# Story Summaries

Although each novel is a self-contained story, to enhance your enjoyment, I highly recommend that you read Books One through Three first. Book One is available as a free download.

## A Reminder of What Happened in Book One

After her husband's death, Josephine Bartlett is moved into the Brookside Retirement Community by her son. Josephine is well on her way to both feeling and acting miserable when she meets Lillian Fitzel, who has nicknamed the place Babbling Brook in honor of the missing waterway and some of the more irritating residents.

Like the unhappy parrot stationed in the lobby, Josephine is liable to bite until Lill begins to smooth her out. Although Josephine accepts Lill as a friend, she avoids having people over because hanging in her living room is an Edward Hopper painting worth millions.

Josephine and Lill are invited to join a foursome to play cards. Finding the usual games dull, Josephine suggests they play strip poker, and Lill morphs that suggestion into what they end up calling naked poker: the person ending the afternoon with the fewest paper clips has to tell a personal story. Something down and dirty so the others won't forget.

Josephine's story is that when her husband wouldn't allow her to work, she scrimped on the household budget and used that money to buy stocks. When her husband discovered her activities, he forced her to turn everything over to him. She secretly rebuilt her holdings until she now has sufficient resources she doesn't need any help from her son, who controls her husband's estate.

Through their naked-poker partners, Josephine and Lill learn that Eddie Colter, a Brookside aide and the resident hunk, is stealing from residents by shorting their change when he shops for them. Eddie, or perhaps someone else, is also stealing valuable items from residents.

Josephine also becomes friends with the young woman who is the associate activities director at Brookside, Devi Subramanian. Devi, previously a curator at the Winterford Art Institute in Chicago, had to leave Chicago after an altercation with her fiancé ended in his accidental death. The police asked Devi not to leave the area until their investigation was complete. However, when the fiancé's brother, Harry Garrison, threatened to kill Devi in revenge, she fled and ended up in Cincinnati.

Given her art background, when Devi sees Josephine's painting, she instantly recognizes it, annoying and worrying Josephine. However, from that contentious beginning, the two eventually develop a warm relationship.

When Josephine and Devi go to the police to report the Brookside thefts, they meet Detective Darren McElroy. Although Mac tells them he can't do much to help unless someone directly connected to the missing items files a report, he does agree to speak to Eddie Colter after both women express concerns for their safety.

Subsequently, Mac becomes friends with Josephine, Devi, and Lill. Divorced two years, he finds himself increasingly attracted to Devi, and his friendship with the three women alleviates his loneliness. Devi is also attracted to Mac, but knows it's best, given what happened in Chicago, to keep her distance.

Once the thefts are officially reported, Mac investigates but makes little progress. Lill, a Graphoanalyst, suggests to Josephine they might be able to identify the thief by analyzing handwriting samples. The two collect samples by telling everyone they are putting together inspirational messages for Eddie's daughter, who supposedly has cancer. In truth, Eddie doesn't have a daughter, but that was his excuse when confronted with his grocery shortfalls.

When the book and a ceremonial check for a fund established by another resident are presented to Eddie, he's furious and blames Devi, whom he ambushes and attacks. Devi fights back, and since she has a black belt in tae kwon do, Eddie comes off the worse from their encounter. That leads him to claim Devi was the aggressor, and he sues her.

Meanwhile, Lill has identified a suspect for the thefts, Edna Prisant, one of the naked-poker ladies. Before that can be investigated further, Josephine's son visits her unexpectedly. He discovers the Edward Hopper painting and spreads the word about its presence.

After Mac and Josephine move the Hopper painting to safety and Josephine hangs another painting in its place, Lill lures Edna into stealing the painting. Edna teams up with Eddie to first drug Josephine and then to remove the painting (not the Hopper) and hide it under Josephine's bed. Edna then calls and demands a ransom.

During the ransom payoff, Edna is apprehended and confesses to the theft of the other missing items. Her explanation is she wanted to help her granddaughter afford a good university. Eddie is implicated as her accomplice in the painting removal, but the evidence is circumstantial.

Harry Garrison then arrives on the scene, and after stalking Devi, takes a shot at her in front of a bakery where Mac and his neighbor, a five-year-old with Down Syndrome, are having a snack. Mac manages to stop Harry from taking a second shot, but the first seriously wounds Devi.

While Mac is at the hospital with Devi, who has barely survived, Lill calls to tell him Josephine is missing. Reluctantly leaving Devi's side, Mac calls his partner for help, and the two discover Josephine has been admitted to a psychiatric facility by her son, who wants to take control of her money.

They manage to break her out, but since she's been drugged, she's admitted to the hospital and ends up as Devi's roommate for the night.

During that night, Josephine tells Devi about the man she loved and should have left her husband for, and she pleads with Devi not to let her chance with Mac slip away.

When Mac takes Devi home from the hospital, Devi follows Josephine's advice and makes the first move to let Mac know she cares for him.

# Book Two

Devi and Mac are falling in love when Mac's ex-wife, Lisa, shows up on Mac's doorstep on a winter evening claiming she needs a place to stay for a "few" days until her new apartment is ready.

Those few days are only the beginning of Mac and Devi's troubles. Lisa is pregnant. At first, she tells Mac it's the result of an affair. Only later does she admit that she had embryos implanted that were created when she and Mac were married. Later still, she admits she's carrying twins. Since Devi is unable to have children, having a pregnant Lisa back in Mac's life is not easy for her. Then Lisa complicates things further by asking for child support. Mac counters with a request for joint custody.

Meanwhile at Brookside, Josephine and Lillian have made a new friend, Philippa, a former attorney now a novelist, and her husband, Richard. Also new on the scene is Devi's temporary replacement, a man named Norman Neumann who seems interested in Josephine.

When everyone plays matchmaker for Josephine and Norman, she has him investigated and discovers he's not the former forensic accountant he claims to be. Instead, he is a partner in a firm that recovers lost art and antiquities. Eventually, Josephine learns he suspects she might have been involved in a museum heist that took place in Boston forty years ago. An Edward Hopper painting was taken, and since Josephine lived in Boston at that time and has an Edward Hopper painting, it's the strongest lead Norman's had in years.

Josephine takes him to the Cincinnati Art Museum to prove her painting is being stored there and is not the one that was stolen. With that settled, Norman decides to pursue a relationship with Josephine, but she makes it clear she's happy on her own. When Norman leaves his temporary undercover position at Brookside, he and Josephine lose touch.

After Devi recovers from being shot, instead of returning to Brookside, she accepts a position at the Cincinnati Art Museum, funded by a grant from Josephine. Lillian, Josephine, and Philippa put together a workshop on how to avoid scams and cons, and Lillian puts her Graphoanalyst skills to work to help Edna Prisant, the Brookside thief, become a better person. Lillian also informs Josephine she has caution strokes in her handwriting that might indicate a reticence that could have held her back from accepting Norman's offer of friendship.

At the museum gala to welcome her Edward Hopper painting, Josephine encounters Norman. Seeing him with another woman, who turns out to be his daughter, Josephine realizes she has missed him and is sorry she sent him away. Josephine and Norman begin to repair their relationship.

After the gala, Lisa gives birth, and Devi and Mac find themselves taking care of one of the newborns while Lisa and the other twin remain in the hospital. When she's released from the hospital, Lisa is quickly overwhelmed caring for both babies, and begs Mac for help. He and Devi step in, and the three of them begin to share the care of the twins.

Because of the twins, Mac and Devi put off their wedding until November. Josephine serves as chief planner, and the novel ends with the wedding.

## *Book Three*

There's a new resident at Brookside Retirement Community (Charlotte, call me Lottie) Watson. She tells an intriguing naked poker story of how she lost her husband in the LA airport many years previously.

Lillian and Josephine are intrigued, and although Lottie shows little interest in what happened to her husband, Josephine is determined to find out. As she and Lillian dig into Lottie's past, Mac's past in the form of his ex-wife, Lisa continues to cause difficulties.

When Lisa gets engaged, both Devi and Mac become concerned about what will happed with their custody arrangement with Lisa. Then Lisa gets married, her husband is transferred to Japan for two years, and she informs them she's taking the twins with her. Mac decides not to fight Lisa's decision despite its effect on Devi.

Then Lisa asks Devi to fly to Japan with her to help with settling in the twins, and Devi agrees. Shortly after their arrival in Japan, Lisa falls seriously ill and has to be hospitalized. It's discovered she's pregnant, but suffering from a severe form of morning sickness that's likely to continue for months. She and her husband decide to ask Devi to take the twins home to Cincinnati, a decision that brings much joy to Devi and Mac.

Meanwhile, Josephine's investigator discovers that Lottie was never married, but she did have a wealthy aunt and uncle named Charlotte and Clarence Watson. After Clarence died, Lottie came to live with her aunt, and less than two years later, the aunt died, apparently after having transferred all her assets to Lottie.

Josephine and Lill suspect that Lottie scammed Charlotte out of her estate and then, in some way, hastened her aunt's death, although that's going to be difficult, if not impossible, to prove. A complication is that Lottie has set her sights on Norman, and when she learns he's in California doing a security audit at the Getty, she travels there and "happens to run" into him. She returns to Cincinnati with him, something Josephine learns when she picks him up at the airport. Norman further muddies the waters by taking Lottie to dinner. He's seeking more information from her, hoping to surprise Josephine, but all he succeeds in doing is getting Lottie drunk and upsetting Josephine.

As Norman and Josephine work through their misunderstandings, more details about Lottie's potential scamming of her aunt are uncovered. As a ploy, Josephine, Lill, and Philippa set up a meeting with Lottie to talk about updating a scams and cons workshop they've given in the past. They ply Lottie with wine and get her to talk hypothetically about how a person could take over an elderly relative's life. Josephine is absolutely convinced Lottie is telling them how she took over her aunt's life, but the problem remains how to prove it.

Lottie has only hazy memories of the party, but begins to suspect Josephine is looking into her past. She decides she needs to get rid of Josephine, and what better way than to doctor her tea with oleander, the same technique she used on her aunt. She adds oleander leaves to Josephine's tea and waits for Josephine to make a cup and drink it.

Before that happens, Richard, Philippa's husband and a former conman himself, hatches a plan to flush Lottie out. He visits her to do a private beer tasting...bringing beer that has been doctored. A drunk Lottie admits she conned her aunt, but declares nothing can be done because the statute of limitations has run out. When Richard and Philippa go to report to Josephine, they find her passed out. Remembering Lottie talking about oleander, they suspect Josephine has been poisoned. That suspicion leads to Josephine receiving prompt treatment with an antidote.

Lottie is now on the hook for attempted murder. And when she discovers the statute of limitations on the con has not expired, since the clock on that actually started once the con was discovered by Josephine, she goes berserk and attacks Mac, adding more charges against her.

With the Lottie affair successfully disposed of, Josephine is ready to fully reconcile with Norman. She asks him to marry her, and he does.

## *And Now You're Ready for Book Four*

If you enjoy reading The Babbling Brook Naked Poker Club novels, I hope you'll consider writing a brief review. Having a minimum number of reviews is a prerequisite for me to be able to publicize these novels on book-discovery sites. Reviews need not be elaborate. Although longer reviews are preferred, even a brief statement of your opinion helps prospective readers decide whether to download the book(s).

# Chapter One

## Josephine

Norman and I were in the final throes of moving into our new home, a three-bedroom-plus-den cottage that's part of the Brookside Retirement Community. Norman's dubbed it *A Cottage for our Dotage.* I was in the living room, unpacking a box of books, when a knock sounded, and I found the mailman peering around our partially open front door.

He held out a priority mail envelope, and my first thought was that my son was making another attempt to serve me with some sort of summons. Ever since he discovered I have ample resources, he's been trying to separate me from them.

As I hesitated, Norman appeared and accepted the envelope. He turned toward me, looking at the envelope and frowning.

"What is it?" I asked.

"Not sure."

"Maybe it's a card, congratulating us."

Norman and I have only recently married, and I must admit it feels odd to assume the label of newlywed at seventy-one. But as a result, we are still getting the occasional greeting from some far-flung friend who has just heard the news.

"It's been forwarded from my old address, so I don't expect you know a Leonardo D. Vincent?"

An intriguing name, given Norman's connections to the art world. "Why don't you just open it?"

"When all else fails, including my x-ray vision . . ."

He grinned at me, and after yanking on the easy-open feature, pulled out a piece of paper. He glanced at it, then held it up for me to see. It contained three words written with a black pen that had meandered its way across the page.

### *Elizabeth Kent Oakes*

"Oh." I felt like someone had punched me . . . lightly, but it still knocked the breath out of me. There were few words that would be as evocative for my new husband as the name of the museum in Boston that had artwork worth over one hundred million dollars stolen some forty years ago.

"Indeed," he said.

Norman's biggest professional regret is that he never turned up a viable lead to this particular theft. It caused an inordinate delay in his retirement, and he'd even suspected me, briefly, of being involved.

I wasn't. But I have to admit, there were circumstances that made it appear I could be one of the people he'd been searching for, for so many years.

"What do you think it means?" I asked.

He flipped the paper over, held it up to the light, then turned his attention to the envelope.

"I'm going to check out this address," he said, walking over to the computer.

While he did that, I abandoned the books and made myself a ceremonial first cup of tea in our new home. In between sips, I worked on getting the kitchen in order.

Norman came to stand in the doorway. "How do you feel about taking a trip to Indianapolis?"

"You found something?"

"Come see."

I followed him to the computer, which was open to a Google Maps street view of the address on the envelope. On the screen was a huge stone house, more suited to Bavaria than

Indianapolis, peeking from behind a tall hedge and bracketed by large trees.

"Do you know who the owner is?"

"Not Leonardo D. Vincent."

"Then who?"

Norman shook his head, his arm circling my waist. "Unclear. Our best bet may be just to go there."

"Is that an investigative technique?" I was teasing, but Norman answered with a serious expression.

"It's almost always an excellent idea to follow up on a strong lead as quickly as possible."

I had no idea what made this piece of paper with its three wobbly words a strong lead, but I was happy to take a break from the settling-in process, even if it was to go to Indianapolis. Which, I suspect, like Cincinnati does better as a place to live rather than a place to visit. My first husband, Thomas, always referred to it as India-no-place. But then, Thomas was a consummate snob.

"A quick trip to Indianapolis, hmm? If nothing else, seeing inside that . . . edifice should be interesting. When do you want to go?" I leaned my head on his shoulder, and to my delight, got a kiss for my effort.

"Right now might be good."

"That's impulsive."

A quick squeeze, and he released me. "I have a feeling about this, and I'm glad you're willing to come along."

I didn't say it, but had he tried to go without me, I would have been hurt and disappointed. After all, my recent success unmasking Lottie Watson's crimes gave me the right, in my opinion, to be part of any investigational opportunities that drifted my way. Or Norman's. And it would not have boded well for our future as a married couple had he hesitated in this moment to include me.

Of course, unlike my most recent adventure, I wasn't expecting a trip to Indianapolis to be either as exciting or as dangerous as the Lottie Watson takedown, but one never knows.

"We'd better plan on spending the night," Norman said.

With a feeling of invigorating anticipation, I went off to pack.

~ ~ ~

It was a two-and-a-half-hour drive from Brookside to the Indianapolis address on the mysterious envelope. As promised by Google, we found ourselves in front of a building that would be an excellent candidate for a Halloween haunted house.

The gate guarding entry to the drive was open, so Norman turned in, and we parked in a graveled area on one side of the house. When we got out of the car, the heat and humidity of the late Midwest summer wrapped around us like a heavy cloak.

The bass tone of the doorbell sounded deep within the house, competing with the high-pitched buzzing of cicadas. I was tempted to peer through the ornate glass sidelight but luckily refrained, because within moments, the door opened and a man in jeans and a polo shirt greeted us.

I felt a stab of disappointment. Given the grand facade and the mysterious arrival of the envelope, I was expecting, at the least, a properly attired butler. This man, with his thinning brown hair and slight paunch, was . . . ordinary.

"Can I help you?"

I blinked. The clothing might not be Savile Row, but the accent was.

Norman held up the envelope.

The man glanced at the address. "Ah, yes, Mr. Neuman. And this is?" He raised his chin toward me.

"Mrs. Neuman," Norman replied.

The man nodded. "Of course. Very appropriate. Perhaps you'd follow me?"

No perhaps about it. We weren't going anywhere until we had some answers. Norman ushered me over the threshold ahead of him. Inside, I was met by blessedly cool air. We followed the man past a beautifully carved spiral staircase into a remarkably cheerful and informal room.

Afternoon sun sent slants of light across a glossy floor. The windows lacked drapes, probably for the benefit of the many plants. The room was warmer than the hall, but still cooler than outside. A large painting of a severe man in medieval clothing hanging above a marble fireplace caught my attention.

Norman sucked in an audible breath as he, too, stared at the painting.

The man—I'd decided butler was an appropriate descriptor despite his clothing—also turned. "Ah, perhaps you recognize it?"

Norman nodded. "The Duke of Northumberland. It's currently listed as missing from the Antwerp Museum."

But while Norman recognized the painting, I didn't. I stepped closer, searching for an artist's signature, but I couldn't make one out.

"Mrs. Scott's orders are that if you showed no sign of recognition, I was to serve you tea and fiction before showing you the door."

"But since I did?"

The butler pulled a phone from his pocket and, watching us both, put it to his ear. "Yes, ma'am. He has the envelope, and he recognized the painting. There's a Mrs. Neuman with him." He paused, obviously listening. "Yes, ma'am. Right away."

The phone was slipped back into his pocket, and he gestured for us to sit in two chairs pulled up to a low table. He disappeared briefly before returning with a large tray containing a tea service that would not have looked out of place in Buckingham Palace.

"Please, help yourselves to tea. Mrs. Scott will be with you shortly."

As soon as the man left the room, I turned to Norman. "What's all that about the painting?"

"I've been investigating its disappearance almost as long as I have the paintings taken in the Boston robbery."

"You think we've entered the den of a master thief?"

His lips twitched. "Quite possibly. Although he, or she, needs to take better care than to hang a priceless masterpiece in such a bright room."

"Perhaps it's a temporary gig for the duke? Or maybe a copy. Cup of tea?"

"Not for me, thank you. But go ahead. I'm sure you're curious."

"I am wondering what kind of tea would be worthy of such a grand pot." I poured myself a cup, took a sip, and with a shudder, set the cup down.

"What's wrong?"

"An inferior brew. Not at all what I was expecting."

The door on the opposite side of the room opened, and the butler pushed a woman in a wheelchair into position across the table from Norman and me. The woman's straight posture and strong profile reminded me of Maggie Smith, a.k.a. the Dowager Countess of Grantham from *Downton Abbey*. Had she been much younger and had walked in, I have no doubt she could have done so with books or a pitcher of water balanced perfectly on her head.

Her hair was white and held back from her face by two jeweled combs. Her fingers were twisted, and her skin was wrinkled and spotted. But her eyes were alert, and their probing gaze locked in on Norman.

The functionary exited the room, leaving the three of us to examine each other.

After the door closed, Mrs. Scott's head inclined slightly. "It's nice to see you again, Norman Neuman. And you're Mrs. Neuman? What is your name?" Her accent matched that of the polo-shirted butler.

I cleared my throat, surprised at being addressed. "Josephine."

"I see you've tried the tea. Would you pour me a cup, please, Josephine?"

"It's not very good tea." Her demeanor and those sharp eyes made my announcement seem perfectly reasonable.

She laughed while Norman gave me a puzzled look. "Don't pour me any, then. You're not a tea drinker, Norman?"

"I prefer coffee."

"Of course you do. But you haven't come to discuss beverage preferences with me, have you."

Norman shook his head, then simply sat without speaking, so I curbed my tongue as well. This was his scene, after all. I was just lucky to have been included.

I could already imagine describing it for Philippa. She's a novelist, and since she found inspiration in my Edward Hopper painting troubles and the Lottie Watson affair, I know she'd find this situation equally fraught with creative possibility.

Mrs. Scott's hands tightened on the cane lying across her lap, and she pulled in a breath. It was the first sign that she wasn't completely calm and in control of the situation. But then she seemed to change her mind and turned once again to me. "How old are you, Josephine?"

Since turning seventy, not to mention moving to Brookside where I live among people who are decades older than I am, I no longer have any particular objection to this question. "Nearly seventy-two. And you?"

"How old do you think I am?"

I pursed my lips, then figured, *Why not?* "One hundred and two."

She laughed, the sound more musical than I was expecting. Then she nodded at me, her eyes alight with humor, her hands more relaxed. "You're not off by much."

"So, you're only . . . ninety-two?"

"Something close to that."

"Still impressive."

Norman shifted, and I took that to mean he was ready to get to the point. And it wasn't to compare ages any more than it was about beverage preferences.

Mrs. Scott noticed as well and turned her attention to him. "I know. You're thinking, 'Get on with it, already.'"

"Yes," Norman said.

"You're right. You've been summoned, and your prompt appearance has earned you an explanation. We contacted two individuals in an identical manner. Since you're the first to arrive, you're the one we'll work with."

I was busy doing some math. The Boston robbery mentioned in the note was perpetrated over forty years ago by three physically agile thieves. This woman would have been at least fifty at that time. Too old to have participated in the robbery itself. Probably. But then Norman's theory, which matched that of the authorities, was that it was a work for hire.

While my mind took this detour, Mrs. Scott said, "I remember that you spent some time in this area about thirty years ago, investigating a stolen painting. We even met, although I doubt you remember."

Norman nodded. "No, I believe I do. At an art museum affair. The director said you were a major patron? Your name was something unusual . . . not Scott."

"I was Agatha Peridot then. And I am a great art lover. Which is what first attracted me to Stanley."

"Stanley?"

"Stanley Scott. My husband. And may I say, I was hoping you'd arrive first. He bet Malcolm Johannsen would."

"The paintings are here?" Norman rarely lets a conversation wander from the point for long without gently redirecting. It's one of the things I admire about him.

"Why don't I give you a tour? If you wouldn't mind pushing me to the entrance hall, there's an elevator located behind the staircase."

I didn't ask permission to accompany them. For one thing, I had no intention of being left alone in the house of what might turn out to be a criminal. So I walked ahead of Norman to open the door. Once in the hall, Agatha directed us to a spot facing the wood-paneled wall behind the staircase. She reached out with her cane and tapped on part of a carving, and a panel opened to reveal an elevator.

"The two of you will need to wait here until the elevator returns," she said.

Once she was inside, the panel slid shut and a mechanical whirring followed.

"You don't think there's any danger, do you?" I asked Norman. The house was spooky, even if Agatha seemed to be a nice old lady. But old ladies were not always as nice as they appeared to be. Something I knew from experience.

He shook his head. "They invited me here. I very much doubt it was to do me harm."

To distract myself, I examined the carving and committed to memory the spot that opened the panel. Then I stepped over to the staircase and ran my fingers over the intricate carvings of birds and flowers. I wondered how they'd found an artisan to do this kind of work. Although . . . the staircase could have been brought over from Europe. But adding the carving masking the elevator had to have been more recent.

The elevator returned, the panel opened, and we entered. There was only one button, and when we pressed it, the panel closed. Norman seemed totally relaxed. Nervously, I counted the seconds of our descent and reached ten before the elevator jerked to a halt. We stepped into a dimly lit space where Agatha awaited us. I glanced around to verify there was nobody else present.

"What period of art interests you the most?" Agatha asked Norman.

"The seventeenth century."

"Ah, straight to the point, I see, although we have other periods that may be of equal interest to you. But the seventeenth century, it is. That will be that area there." She pointed her cane toward a darkened alcove to the right.

As we approached, recessed lights in the ceiling came on, and as their glow intensified, the paintings, at least ten of them, emerged from the gloom. I glanced back at Agatha to reassure myself she wasn't heading for the elevator, leaving us in what appeared to be a place with no other exits.

Norman, looking completely at ease, strolled from one painting to the next. I tried to stop worrying and moved close enough to each painting to search out the artist's signature. I managed to recognize several of the names. Norman gave me a slight nod, which I took to mean at least some of these works were the paintings he'd been searching for most of his professional life. I could imagine his elation, although he was doing a good job of keeping it under wraps.

We returned to Agatha, and Norman said, "Not all of those are from the Boston museum heist."

"Of course not. Stanley acquired art over many decades and from many sources. Would you like to see more?"

"What about the twentieth century?"

"Over there." She pointed to the left. Another dim alcove.

The lights came on, and I spotted the Edward Hopper painting immediately. As my gaze moved from painting to painting, I recognized two by Andrew Wyeth and one by Winslow Homer. With the quiet and the indirect lighting, it was like visiting a museum, a feast for both the eyes and the imagination.

Like me, Norman gazed around the area before he moved closer to the paintings. I wanted to ask him if the Hopper was the one taken in the Boston heist, then decided to ask Agatha, who seemed to be in a sharing frame of mind.

"Of course it is," she said in response to my query. "Stanley gave it to me as a wedding present. I didn't realize it was stolen until recently."

"Why are you telling us this?" I asked. It seemed silly to drag out this elaborate dance any further.

"Perhaps that would be easier to explain if I add Stanley to the conversation."

We followed Agatha back upstairs, and I was very much relieved to step out of the elevator onto the main floor. There, she directed our steps in the opposite direction from the cheerful conservatory into a part of the house that was darker, more foreboding. We arrived at a closed door, and Agatha tapped with her cane.

The door was opened by the butler. He ushered the three of us inside a large room furnished with a hospital bed and medical accoutrements. The occupant of the room, attired in a maroon smoking jacket, sat in a recliner near the windows. His face was gaunt and pale, and his body appeared shrunken, but when he smiled at Agatha, I could imagine him as a younger, healthier man.

At Agatha's direction, Norman parked her chair near the man. She leaned over to take his hand in hers. His other hand was propped on a cane that I doubted, given his obvious fragility, was ever used for walking. My uneasy feelings about the house and the Scotts dissipated completely.

"It went well?" he asked in a wheezy voice that had clearly been altered by advancing age and illness.

"Very well. Stanley, this is Norman and Josephine Neuman."

"Ah. You've won your bet, then."

Agatha gestured for us to sit on chairs the butler pushed into place. Once we did, Stanley, with an obvious effort, tipped his head up and examined us. Then his head returned to its former bent position. I wondered if he was in constant pain from holding his head that way.

Agatha waited until the door had closed behind the butler before speaking. "Stanley and I would be interested in knowing what conclusions the two of you have drawn."

I sat, my hands folded, waiting for Norman to speak.

He nodded at Stanley and Agatha, his lips pursed. "I've just been shown most of the paintings stolen from the Elizabeth Kent Oakes Museum forty-three years ago. And since you summoned me here, I'm guessing you want my help in returning them to their rightful place."

"What's your thinking about the other works you saw?" Stanley spoke with obvious effort, again lifting his head briefly.

"Three of the paintings in your twentieth-century area have also been reported as stolen. And there's the portrait of the duke in the conservatory. Perhaps you're considering the return of those as well?"

"You have an excellent memory, Norman Neuman." Stanley stopped to catch his breath. "Perhaps you might make a guess about my diagnosis."

Norman shook his head. "I leave medical issues to the appropriate practitioners."

"Diplomatically put. Agatha, my dear, would you like to do the honors? After all, this is your idea."

"You're correct in thinking Stanley and I wish to return the artwork stolen from the Elizabeth Kent Oakes Museum. But we want it done quietly, without fanfare, and without revealing our role."

"I doubt that's possible," Norman said. "It was a huge sensation when the art was stolen. Its return will be a major story."

Stanley and Agatha exchanged a glance that I was unable to fully decipher, but was possibly a mix of "I told you so," overlaid with something that could have been, "Okay, it's plan B then." But perhaps I was being fanciful.

"Can you at least assure us that you'll keep this location a secret?" Stanley said.

"If I'm unable to grant such assurances, what will happen to the art?"

Agatha shrugged. "We have buyers lined up. If you don't keep us out of it, we'll ensure that the art disappears again, and this time, it will be for good."

"I could leave here and call the FBI."

"If any FBI agents show up, we have contingency plans to destroy the paintings. Could you live with that outcome?"

I didn't believe her, and I doubted Norman did either. Clearly, the two loved art too much to harm it. But the threat could be an indication of how desperate they were for our help.

"How do you suggest we do this, then?" Norman said, obviously coming to the same conclusion I had.

"Do you give us your word?" Stanley leaned forward, then gasped with apparent pain.

"I promise to do all I can to keep your names and your location confidential," Norman said.

"We will also need your promise of confidentiality, my dear." Stanley twisted to give me a quick glance.

I turned to Norman, who nodded slightly.

"I will honor your confidence as far as it is in my power to do so," I said, meeting Agatha's gaze. I crossed my fingers and silently added the words "from this day on," since I'd already told Lill and Devi about the trip, and even given Devi the address.

Lill is my best friend at Brookside. She's the one who said it should be called Babbling Brook, a tongue-in-cheek reference to the lack of a brook and the presence of garrulous residents. As for Devi, she and I met when she was the Brookside activities director. And I doubt either of us would have bet a nickel we'd be friends after our first meeting. But Devi and I have been through tough times together, and we now treasure our relationship, despite a forty-year difference in our ages.

"Good. Glad to hear it." Stanley sat back, taking quick, shallow breaths.

Norman might not want to hazard a medical guess, but mine was that Stanley had advanced congestive heart failure. That's what killed my first husband, whose symptoms had been similar. And Stanley's symptoms were so severe, I doubted he'd be alive in six months. As for Agatha, despite her upright posture and determined cheerfulness, she also appeared fragile. In the slanted light from the window, her skin had a yellow tinge that might indicate she had a liver condition.

Poor health and advancing years were likely why the two were now making arrangements to return the paintings. I wondered if they had any heirs waiting in the wings to swoop in and take over their collection. That might need looking into.

"How do you plan to handle the return?" Norman asked.

"We're going to arrange for the transfer of the art to an intermediate location, which we'll share with you within two months' time," Stanley said.

"You'd better give us your phone number to make the final arrangements," Agatha said.

"Certainly." Norman accepted the paper and pen Agatha handed him and wrote down both our home and cell phone numbers.

"Excellent," Stanley said with another quick bob of his head.

Then he exchanged a look with Agatha, and a moment later, the butler reappeared to escort us out.

On a whim, I turned to him when we reached the front door and offered my hand. "It was nice to meet you, Mr. Vincent."

He shook his head, ignoring my hand. "Sorry, ma'am. That's not me." Then he reached around me, opened the door, and ushered us firmly out.

"Nice try," Norman said after we were in the car. "But he didn't fall for it."

"So . . . do you think there really is a Leonardo D. Vincent?"

"I suspect Agatha made him up."

"Maybe the butler's her son? I mean, he called her 'Mum.'"

"He's a Brit. I think he was saying 'ma'am.' Which is also what he called you."

"O . . . kay. Do you think they'll return the art?"

"I believe that's their intention," Norman said. "But we'll just have to wait and see."

~ ~ ~

Leaving the Scotts, we decided we'd rather sleep in our own bed, even though it would be late by the time we got home.

"Isn't this a bit crazy?" I asked Norman. "I mean, we could have loaded the paintings into the car and taken them back to Cincinnati today."

"We're talking about the return of paintings worth millions, Jo. I'm okay with doing it whatever way Agatha and Stanley decide is most comfortable for them."

"But how long do we give them? Two months? Really? Don't you think we better call the FBI?"

"We gave our word, and I think they have every intention of holding up their end. Remember, they contacted us. And I certainly don't want to take any chances on the paintings being sold or harmed, even if I think that's unlikely."

An ugly possibility occurred to me. "And you risk not earning your finder's fee if we don't play it their way."

Norman's substantial net worth came from what insurance companies have paid him for the return of stolen art. And art valued at over one hundred million dollars would involve a very nice payday.

"There is a substantial reward, or at least there was one. I seem to remember there was a time limit placed on it. But for me, the satisfaction comes from knowing what happened to the art and being involved, however peripherally, in its return."

Since he was driving, I turned and examined him closely as he spoke, searching for any telltale signs he was lying to either himself or to me. I didn't see any.

"They said nothing about what will become of the other pieces you recognized as being stolen. Do you think they'll return them as well?"

"I have no idea. I'm taking whatever I can get. At least as a first step."

"Why are they involving us, do you think? And moving the paintings to a secondary location? How are they going to manage that?"

"My guess is the butler will help them. And I don't know why they've involved us. Maybe they want to avoid being charged with a crime, although that's unlikely since the statute of limitations has expired for the original burglary. Or perhaps it's a legacy issue. They're hoping to maintain the fiction that they're legitimate collectors and art patrons."

"Their reputations won't matter much once they're dead. And I agree with you, that will be sooner rather than later."

"All the more reason to trust they'll go through with this."

"And us. Do you mean to tell me, we can't ever talk about this, or how it came about, to anyone else? After all, even attorney-client privilege ends at death."

"Let's worry about that later."

But what worried me was that I'd already mentioned the envelope with its cryptic message to both Lill and Devi.

I told Devi so she and her husband, Mac, who's a police detective, would know where we were going. Just in case. Given what's happened to me the past couple of years when I didn't keep Mac fully informed—a drugging, an abduction, and a poisoning—I thought it made sense. Not that I expected that sort of excitement this time, especially since meeting the Scotts.

As for Lill, she isn't a gossip, but I didn't ask her to keep the information to herself. Which meant she could mention it to someone like Edna, who could easily tell Myrtle, and if it were passed on to Myrtle, it wouldn't be surprising to find it being reported on the six o'clock news.

I knew keeping that information from Norman was a very bad idea. I'd had over seventy years to learn that even small omissions or commissions can have far-reaching consequences, and so I took a deep breath and told him what I'd done.

His hands tensed momentarily, then relaxed. "That's okay. Not a problem, love. Just maybe ask Lill not to say anything about it to anyone else."

I realized I'd tensed as well, expecting to be scolded, because that's what my first husband would have done. Norman's reaction was yet another sign I'd gotten it right the second time around.

# Chapter Two

## Devi

Mac arrived home and received his usual enthusiastic greeting from Lily and Toby, who race each other to be the first to reach him. It's still a crawling race, but they'll be walking before long.

Mac lifted one twin after the other, giving each a twirl that left them gurgling with delight, then he turned to give me my kiss. As always, it made my heart skip and my lips curve in a smile.

"Josephine called," I told him, once the twins settled down. "She and Norman left for Indianapolis this afternoon."

"What for?"

"To follow up on a clue."

Mac rolled his eyes. "Josephine. Plus a clue. I see paperwork in my future."

He was teasing. Josephine's investigations may be amateur, but they've helped him root out a couple of thieves and unmask a murderer whose victim had been thought to have died from natural causes.

Mac is a detective with the Montgomery, Ohio, police force, while I work at the Cincinnati Art Museum as the curator of special projects. Josephine pays my salary through a grant, and since Mac and I adopted the twins, she grants me as much time off as I need.

"So, what was the clue?"

"An address that accompanied a sheet of paper with the words *Elizabeth Kent Oakes* on it. And I assume she told me in case they drop out of sight."

Mac's startled expression changed to a grin. "You know, a year ago, she'd have gone off, probably with Lillian in tow, to check things out without telling anyone."

"This time she's with Norman, and he is a trained investigator. So you're right, it's a definite improvement."

And sharing information about the trip was further proof that Josephine meant it when she said she now considers us, along with Lillian, members of her family. We're an odd mix. Lillian is African American, and my dad is from India. Mac is the only one of us who looks like he might actually be related to Josephine. Doesn't matter. We are, in every sense of the word, family.

"Do you think she'll keep us informed?" Mac asked.

"No idea," I said, handing him silverware and dinner plates.

We're house-sitting a mini-mansion, actually not so mini, while the owners sail around the world. Although we've chosen to live mostly in the mother-in-law suite, baby equipment is now scattered farther afield.

"Back to the subject of Josephine and Norman," I said as I set down the casserole I'd made for dinner. "It would be terrific if the two of them discover something about the Elizabeth Kent Oakes heist."

Mac nodded. "Yeah, I agree."

He ate quickly because we never get to sit long while Lily and Toby are awake. As he picked up his empty plate to carry it over to the sink, I was still thinking about Josephine and Norman's Indianapolis quest.

I knew Norman had to be thrilled to have what could be a solid clue. He'd regaled us one evening with some of his adventures during the past forty years of searching for the thieves. One notable misstep was the time he suspected Josephine might have had a role in the robbery, and he spent several weeks as Brookside's associate activities director, my former position, in order to investigate her. Instead of finding an art thief, he found love . . . the best red herring of his career, according to him.

If he and Josephine found and returned the art, he'd be feted by the entire museum community since that theft altered the approach to security in every museum worldwide. That might make this Josephine's most thrilling adventure yet.

The thought left me a bit uneasy, though. There could be dangers as well as answers lying in wait in Indianapolis, although danger was unlikely.

But then Josephine has encountered unlikely danger before.

~ ~ ~

"I had lunch with Josephine today," I told Mac when he arrived home the next evening.

"What did she have to say about Indianapolis?"

"According to her, a complete bust."

"Do I hear doubt in your voice?"

"She seemed nervous when I asked her about it. And the whole thing sounded odd. After they rushed off with five minutes' notice, why would they let a little thing like nobody answering the door deter them?"

"The Jo moves in mysterious ways."

"You're not taking this seriously."

"Maybe not. But Norman and Jo are still newlyweds. Taking a quick trip to somewhere, being spontaneous, it's part of the package."

"Is it? And when was the last time we were spontaneous, Darren McElroy?" I planted my hands on my hips and raised my chin in challenge. "After all, we're newlyweds too." Although, I will admit it isn't easy being spontaneous while balancing the care of twins with our demanding careers. But it's not impossible.

Which Mac demonstrated by pulling me into his arms for a very thorough kiss. When he lifted his head, I blinked at him, dazed.

He ran a finger over my cheek and touched my lips. "See, we've still got it too." And I suspect if it weren't for the fact we had two babies tottering around our feet, he would have swooped me up right then and there and had his way with me.

Later, after the twins were in bed, and we were as well, I spooned up against Mac. "I think something's going on."

"With Norman and Jo?"

"Yes. If you'd been there, I think you'd agree with me."

"Jo does have a penchant for getting into trouble. What are you going to do?"

"There isn't much I can do, although . . ."

"What?"

"Josephine said the whole thing could be a practical joke, and that Norman was checking to find out who owned the house."

"And?"

"We could do that too. Check on the owners, I mean."

"I see where you're going. You get the names, and then you'll want me to run them through the system."

"Something like that."

"You know I can't do that. But whatever you find out in the civilian universe is fair game."

We were silent a couple of minutes, then I asked the other question that had been bugging me, ever since Mac recently shared that he was being considered for the chief of police position in Loveland.

"What about the chief's job? We haven't talked about it."

"What do you want to know?"

"Are you really interested?"

"Not sure yet."

I turned to face him. "Just so you know, it's okay if you want to change jobs. And I know it's unrealistic to demand you share your every thought, but we should discuss major stuff."

"Like job changes. I agree. I was wrong to keep it to myself as long as I did."

"And?" I said.

He smiled. "It won't happen again."

I gave him a playful dig in the ribs. "It better not, Darren McElroy, or you might find yourself sleeping on the couch." Since there are at least ten couches and another six or so recliners in the main part of the house, his only difficulty would be picking one. And being separated from me.

Something neither one of us has wanted to be since I almost died after being shot by my former fiancé's brother.

## Chapter Three

### *Edna*

"And then Fiona the baby hippo blew a huge raspberry right at Billy and Adam. They jumped back, laughing. It was their best zoo visit ever."

I looked down at the circle of faces surrounding me. Both boys and girls were grinning in delight.

I confess, I've enjoyed my community service much more than I had any right to. My sentence was two hours a week for a year, helping out at the local library. I was being punished, rightfully so, for trying to steal Josephine's painting and actually stealing some things from other people in the retirement community where I live. And I do realize I got off light.

I was not a very nice person back then. Lillian Fitzel helped me improve my character with something she calls Graphotherapy. How it worked was she pointed out something in my handwriting for me to change. Then I practiced until the change she'd suggested became automatic. Her first suggestion was that I slant my lines of writing up rather than down. After I'd been doing that for several weeks, I noticed I felt more positive than I had in years.

One other surprising thing to come out of my legal difficulties, besides the Graphotherapy and the community service, has been that Josephine and I have become friends. I realized I'd been elevated to friendship status when she gave me a package of exotic tea for my birthday. Josephine only gifts people she likes with tea.

I wonder if she's ever given any to Myrtle? I can't ask, of course. If she has, it might make me less certain Josephine considers me a friend. And if she hasn't, I might slip into a feeling of superiority, which would definitely slow my progress in improving my character.

Happily, most people have now forgotten my misdeeds. That's a major benefit of living with old people. We don't have the memory or the time to hold grudges.

~ ~ ~

"Edna Prisant. I do not understand why you've become such a snob," Myrtle Grabinowitz said, spotting me when I arrived at bingo night.

When I'd seen her, I'd altered my course toward the other side of the room, but that, unfortunately, wasn't going to work. She gave the place on the sofa next to her a commanding pat.

Bracelets clanked, and the excess fabric in her magenta top swirled around her as she shifted to accommodate me. "Just because you're pals with Josephine now is no reason to act all high and mighty with me."

I sat down without responding, hoping that would shush her. No such luck.

"Don't forget I stood by you when you were a thief. And don't think for one minute, I've forgotten."

"Of course not, Myrtle. Everyone knows you have the memory of an elephant." I struggled not to let an image of an elephant dressed in a magenta tutu overwhelm me. My rule is always to remain courteous and sober toward Myrtle, even when she chooses to refresh everyone's recollection of my misdeeds or tickles my funny bone.

"Well, I just think the two of you haven't been very nice to me lately," Myrtle said. "You might recall, if your memory isn't failing, that I was your friend when everybody else was avoiding you. As for Josephine, nobody liked her either, until I stepped in."

All true. But being friends with Myrtle takes a toll on a person. Her regard is a heavy burden in both the literal and figurative sense.

"I hardly ever see Josephine," I said, going for misdirection rather than outright confrontation. "Not since she and Norman got married."

I laid out my two bingo cards in preparation, hoping that would switch her attention from me to the game. I wished the caller would get on with it, but others were still arriving, shuffling in, leaning on canes and walkers.

"I'm not surprised to hear you say that," Myrtle said, undeterred. "What I don't understand is why they moved into one of those . . . cottages, my foot. Didn't most of us come to Brookside to get away from taking care of a house?"

"I think they have a housekeeper."

"Humph. Of course they do. It's just . . ." She humphed again. "With Josephine gone, there's nobody interesting to play naked poker with."

I glanced around. One or two people were listening, and one of those, a woman with blue-gray hair and clever eyes, didn't look happy about what she was hearing.

"She's not really gone." I lowered my voice, hoping Myrtle would do the same. "Besides, we've already heard one another's stories."

"Well, I don't know about you, but I have a lot more juicy stories I could share. In the spirit of the game. And only if I lose, of course."

"Of course." Inwardly, I shuddered. Myrtle always shares tales of her beauty-pageant days, and while they were interesting the first time around, are not so much in the third and fourth retelling.

However, I *was* trying to be a better person. "Why don't we check with some of the new people and see if they play bridge?"

"Bridge? Fiddle-dee-dee. That's not nearly as much fun as naked poker. I say you and I call on Josephine. I bet we can talk her into a game. And Norman, and maybe Philippa too. You do realize we've never heard their stories."

True. Philippa only played with us once, and since she'd won, or at least she hadn't been the biggest loser, she didn't have to reveal any secrets. And Norman has always slid out of agreeing to play with us. Not that I blame him. I'm quite positive Josephine has warned him. I would certainly have done so, in her shoes.

At that moment, the caller finally pulled the first number, and Myrtle's attention moved away from me.

I placed a marker on one of my cards, deciding as I did so that I had to agree with Myrtle about one thing. Brookside Retirement Community is not nearly as interesting a place to be when Josephine isn't around. She does seem to attract both unusual goings-on and nefarious individuals.

I speak with authority on the latter, since I was so recently one of those nefarious individuals.

# *Chapter Four*

## *Josephine*

In late September, the doorbell rang, and I opened the door to find the mailman placing two large rectangular boxes and two cardboard tubes on our porch. I smiled a thank-you and picked up the tubes, which I carried inside and placed on the dining room table. When I returned to the porch for the remaining boxes, the mailman was already climbing back into his van.

Mentally, I ran through my list of recent online orders and came up blank. Besides, I now saw that the packages had been forwarded from Norman's Indian Hill address. So I did the next best thing—I checked the original address labels. All were written in a spidery hand with an Indianapolis post office box as the return address.

With a tingle of excitement, I opened one of the tubes. It contained a parchment scroll. Carefully, I unrolled the brownish paper, handling it with only the tips of my fingers, and smiled in recognition. It was the da Vinci drawing of a man on a horse I'd last seen framed and hanging on a wall in Agatha and Stanley Scotts' house.

"Yoo-hoo, Josephine."

At the fluty tones, I froze before turning to find Myrtle Grabinowitz in the doorway.

"I knocked, but you didn't come. Your door was unlocked, so I thought I'd just pop in."

Her gaze came to rest on the drawing, which I was holding flat. I lifted my fingers, and it re-rolled itself. Then I took a deep breath, hoping she hadn't gotten a good enough look, or that if she had, she wouldn't know what it was.

"Oh, goodie. Look at all these boxes. Wedding presents? And that drawing, it looked really old. Can I see?"

"It is old. I didn't realize. I shouldn't be handling it without gloves." An understatement. I was blathering, but since that's Myrtle's customary form of communication, I hoped she wouldn't notice. "Did you walk all the way here?"

She shook her head. "Of course not. Philippa's husband was headed out on an errand and very kindly offered to drop me off."

"Lovely. How about I show you around." I placed myself between Myrtle and the table, ushering her out of the dining room and into the kitchen. "A cup of tea?"

"I'd much rather watch you open your presents. Presents are so much fun, don't you agree?"

"I'm going to wait for Norman so we can open them together."

Thank goodness he wasn't due home for a couple of hours. Had he arrived now, I was quite certain Myrtle would insist on a grand opening party, with herself as a key participant. And given what I suspected the rest of the packages contained, that would be a disaster.

I kept Myrtle in the kitchen, feeding her tea and cookies and making inane conversation for fifteen minutes. Which I hoped was long enough for her to forget about my mail delivery.

"Oh, Josephine, those packages almost made me forget. The reason I wanted to see you. I'm putting together a naked poker group, and as the inventor, I just know you'll want to join us." Myrtle reached for the last cookie, then gave me a smile that challenged me to disagree.

Which I would have if my dining table hadn't been loaded down with boxes containing a fortune in stolen art. But in that particular moment, I was prepared to do whatever it took to remove Myrtle from the premises.

"Why don't I give you a ride back?" I asked after conceding her the victory by accepting the naked poker invitation.

"Why, that's so nice of you, Josephine. I must say, Norman Neuman has certainly had a good effect on you." She tittered. "You do realize everyone but Lillian thought you were a dreadful grouch."

I bit my tongue, then smiled. A totally fake smile that I tried to make appear real. "You're absolutely right, Myrtle. Norman has smoothed out my rough edges. And I'm so grateful. Are you ready?"

She nodded, still chewing, and I walked her to my car, making sure on the way out that the front door was locked.

~ ~ ~

I dropped Myrtle off—a major motion picture. She struggled to get out of the car, so I had to get out to assist her. After heaving her to her feet, I turned to make my escape.

"Now don't forget, Josephine. Wednesday at two. Toodle-oo."

I got back in the car and took a deep breath before driving home. When Norman arrived later, I immediately led him into the dining room.

"What's all this?"

"It just arrived from Indianapolis." I pointed at the rolled-up drawing. "Be careful. Are your hands clean?"

He glanced at me before going to wash up and get a pair of gloves. Then he unrolled the drawing. He drew in a sharp breath, then allowed the paper to gently re-roll.

"Is it the da Vinci from the Boston museum?" I asked.

He nodded. Without speaking, he opened the rest of the packages and carefully examined the contents. Each contained a painting or drawing. "There should be four more." He shook his head. "Can you believe they simply put paintings worth millions in the mail? And no insurance."

"I expect it would take the post office to its knees if it had to pay out an insurance claim for what these are worth."

We both stared at the four pictures, probably thinking the same thing. Were there more to come, or was this it? But if this was it, it was still a relief that Agatha and Stanley had come through on at least part of their promise. And earlier than we expected.

I nodded toward the da Vinci. "Myrtle saw that. I doubt she knew what it was, but if she talks about it . . . And you know how she loves to talk."

"What did you do about it?"

"I had to agree to join a group for a naked poker game."

"I appreciate your sacrifice." He smiled at me, then leaned in for a quick kiss. "I guess all you can do is see if she mentions it again."

Which didn't seem like much of a plan. But, unfortunately, I didn't have a better one.

# Chapter Five

## *Maddie*

I was certain Agatha and Stanley Scott weren't my biological parents when I got old enough to realize it required Agatha to have given birth to me when she was over sixty. But Agatha wouldn't tell me anything about where I came from until I went through a particularly rebellious and demanding period as a teenager.

The story she told me then was that she and Stanley found me when they volunteered to help at an adoption event. Agatha said all the other kids were running around, acting crazy, while I'd sat there quietly drawing. When Stanley saw my drawing, he insisted on taking me home. It sounded more like a story about adopting a puppy than a child.

Agatha kept the drawing, or at least she said it was that drawing. When she showed it to me, I could see what had caught Stanley's eye. It wasn't a typical picture one would expect a four-year-old to draw, and seeing it, Agatha said Stanley realized he'd always hoped to find a protégé to share his passion for art with.

What's odd, though, is that I have no memories of ever living anywhere else but with them. And I should have some memory, no matter how faint, of going to live with new parents, especially if I'd done it when I was old enough to draw the picture Agatha claimed I'd drawn.

The part of the story that rang true was the bit about Stanley wanting to share his passion for art with me. For by the time I started school, Stanley had me copying drawings by da Vinci, Michelangelo, and Degas, both praising and critiquing my efforts. When I wasn't drawing, he taught me the fine points, first of painting with watercolors. Then when I was in middle school, he added oils.

Throughout those years, I shared Stanley's studio, where he produced copies of paintings that then became part of our home's furnishings. I once asked Stanley why he didn't paint pictures of his own, and I still remember his answer.

"These paintings are some of the most magnificent achievements of man. In copying them as precisely as possible, I'm entering into a deeply meaningful relationship with the painter, recreating his genius in our modern world."

"But you're a genius too," I told him. "Just think of the wonderful new pictures you could paint."

"Perhaps. But this is my calling. Quite simply, Madeline, it is the most satisfying work I have ever done, or ever hope to do."

I was young enough that this answer satisfied me.

Once I mastered oil and canvas, Stanley initiated a new aspect of my education. He brought out a painting from a storage closet, one I'd never seen hanging on our walls. Since he'd educated me so thoroughly, I knew it wasn't any good.

"You don't want a copy of that, do you?" I'd pointed at the stiff rendering of a bowl of fruit. Possibly Dutch school, but a kindergarten version of that venerable style of painting.

"Of course not. What we want from this painting is the canvas."

"What on earth for? Can't we afford fresh canvas?"

"Of course we can. But this canvas is very special. It was handwoven in the seventeen hundreds. And you're going to use it to create a copy of this." He pulled another painting from the storage area and set it on an easel.

It was a typically Dutch subject. But unlike the first painting, the skill and creative genius of the painter was obvious. A windmill turned its sails against a dark sky, and water reflected a beam of light coming through a break in the clouds. That gleam directed the eye to a tiny figure standing near the windmill.

"Do we clean the canvas? Or should I paint over it?" I said, referring to the bowl of fruit.

"We'll carefully remove some layers of paint before we begin. And then you'll use my special paints."

Up to then, Stanley had never allowed me to touch his special paints, nor had he explained their purpose. I knew only that he used them when he copied certain paintings.

"You will study this painting carefully before you begin," he said. "Take notice of the brushstrokes and consider the mood of the painter as he worked. You will move in close, and then, in your mind, you will move away. And you and the painter will form an alliance that will serve to keep your hand steady throughout. Oh, and after you study it thoroughly, you will turn the painting upside down before you begin to paint."

"Why?" I'd noticed Stanley doing this, but had never asked why he did it.

"It will help you more closely approach the style of the painter, subsuming your personality in order to make a more perfect copy."

I had only a vague idea at the time what subsuming was. Instead, I focused on a more important issue. "Don't I need a costume?"

On occasion, Stanley would show up to paint wearing a flowing white shirt, tight trousers, and boots. When I asked him why, he said that dressing the part of the particular painter put him into closer psychic contact. My childish imagination, nurtured by Gothic mysteries, easily accepted that explanation.

In answer to my question about dressing up, he'd agreed it was an excellent idea, and Agatha had outfitted me with a long velvet skirt and an elaborate necklace.

By the time Stanley assigned me the task of copying the windmill painting, I was beginning to suspect copying wasn't the precise word for what he did—what he was directing me to do. I didn't attempt to define it further, though. I knew only that whatever he called it, Stanley had my full cooperation and participation.

But although I loved Stanley and wanted his approval, I found copying the windmill painting tedious. When I finished, I worked up my courage and told him I wanted to paint pictures of my own.

I'm certain he was disappointed, but he signed me up for classes at the Indiana Art Institute, and never again did he suggest I copy anything. Stanley's praise of my skill when I'd copied the drawings and the windmill painting had been satisfying, but it was even more satisfying to create a painting of my own out of imagination and thin air. And it was easier to paint pictures when I was able to use fresh canvas and brighter pigments, and I didn't have to be so careful about brushstrokes and color matching.

After I finished my degree, in art restoration, Stanley helped me find an internship with the Indianapolis Art Museum as a restorer. It was a simple matter for Agatha and Stanley to arrange such a thing, as they were patrons of the museum. Patrons, I'm quite sure, who were never suspected of forgery.

Of course, I didn't come to the Stanley-as-a-forger conclusion quickly. My certainty about what he was doing came gradually. By the time I fully understood who he was and what he'd possibly done, he was dying.

He'd loved me, and I loved him. A potent combination that has silenced far stronger voices than mine.

~ ~ ~

A week after Stanley's death, Agatha commanded me to purchase a selection of flat boxes and cardboard tubes from a Staples store twenty miles away. "And please, dear, wear a baseball cap, and if you can find something bland in your wardrobe, do wear that."

I dress conservatively for my generation, but wearing the appropriately nondescript costume Agatha requested made me look and feel both unsavory and slightly overweight. Agatha also told me to keep gloves on while purchasing and handling the boxes. All her instructions were odd, but Agatha had rarely asked me to do anything for her, so as these were her wishes, I carried them out to the best of my ability.

After a successful shopping trip, I carried the boxes in and dumped them on the dining room table.

"You haven't touched them, have you?" she asked.

"Nope. Gloves all the way. Had to tell the guy at the cash register I had psoriasis."

"Why would you do that?"

"He said didn't I find it too hot to wear gloves."

"I guess that can't be helped now. What I need you to do next is come up with a return address that will cause the least amount of hassle for the people living there."

"Hassle? Who's going to hassle them?"

"The FBI art recovery unit."

"Oh," I said, the pieces beginning to fall into place.

"We're going to return some stolen art," she said, giving additional weight to my conclusions.

"We seem to be talking about quite a lot of stolen art." I glanced at the pile of boxes. "All stolen from the same place, or are we talking multiple heists?"

"Please, Maddie, the less you know, the better."

"So you're going to do what? Place priceless artwork in these boxes, and then what?"

"Mail it."

"FedEx, UPS?"

"The post office."

"You're putting what I expect will be very expensive art into the hands of the post office?" I didn't say, *are you nuts*, but I sure thought it.

"It's the only way to manage this anonymously."

"Yes, I see that. Did you and Stanley steal the paintings together?"

Her head jerked, and her posture stiffened. "Of course not. I didn't know Stanley back then. And I don't know if these are originals. I don't think I need to mince words with you. You know what Stanley did for a living."

"He stole paintings, created forgeries, and then sold either the original or the forgery?" I said, hazarding a guess.

"I know only that Stanley had his favorites. The ones he copied, but then kept the originals. I'm pretty sure the ones we'll be returning are all originals."

She'd dodged answering me directly, but I let it go.

Agatha took my hand in hers. "I'm sorry, dear. We should have taken care of all this years ago. Not left it on your shoulders. And I'm sorry I let him involve you the way I did. It's just . . . well, it made him so happy to see you growing as an artist. Walking in his footsteps, in a way."

"You mean as a forger?"

"Well, Stanley said you were very good. Not as good as he was, but with practice . . . And he so treasured his time with you, I didn't want to interfere. He loved you very much, you know. And you were always so happy when you were working on a project."

I should have been upset. Especially when I realized the group of paintings we were returning was from one of the most notorious art heists of all time. But I wasn't. Instead, I was intrigued by Agatha's decision to return the paintings, which had definitely not been among the ones hanging in plain sight for me to see—because I would have known, once I took an art history class, what they were. But loving her and Stanley, I was willing to do whatever I could to ensure their return was accomplished successfully.

And anonymously.

## Chapter Six

### *Lillian*

Myrtle was going through one of her periodic convulsions of neighborliness, and insisted I attend a naked poker game she was hosting. She even claimed that Josephine had agreed to come. Since I considered that extremely unlikely, I made my response vague, telling her I'd let her know if I could fit it into my schedule.

She clucked her tongue and waved a hand at me. That always makes her bracelets clank together in a way that sends my hearing aids into apoplectic fits.

"You snooze, you lose," she said with another clattery wave. "I only have a couple of spots still open."

I doubted there'd be a rush on for those openings, but I refrained from saying so and breathed a sigh of relief when she spotted another victim and took off in rapid pursuit.

Later, I gave Josephine a call, and when I mentioned the game, her response flummoxed me.

"Yes. I did agree to be there. And I could use your help."

"Anything at all. Just name it."

Josephine and I have had adventures together, which means I'm in her debt for enlivening my life. So I'm always up for any new caper she suggests. I was afraid all that was over once she married Norman, but based on the worry in her voice, perhaps it isn't. I know I should be concerned for her, but the last time she sounded this vexed, we unmasked a murderer together.

As soon as I hung up with Josephine, I called Myrtle and accepted the invitation.

"Well, lucky for you, I held the spot," Myrtle said with a sniff.

"Who else will be there?" I asked.

"Edna can't make it because she has her community service thingy, and Philippa, as usual, said she had a writing deadline. But that new couple who moved into Josephine's old apartment, they said they'd be delighted to join us."

"Great." I wondered if Josephine knew the couple were invited. Perhaps not, as she isn't the most social of creatures.

She'd said she didn't want to talk about the help she needed on the phone and was on her way over, so I cut the pleasantries with Myrtle short. Josephine arrived a few minutes later.

I made us some tea, using a blend Josephine gave me for my birthday, and we settled in the living room to discuss her problem.

"This is all very hush-hush, you understand," she said.

"I'm excellent at keeping secrets," I told her.

"I know. That's why you're the only one I can talk to about this."

"What about Devi? Have you asked for her help?"

"I can't."

That surprised me. Josephine is very close to Devi. And to Mac. As a matter of fact, she trusted Mac enough to assign him her power of attorney and health-care proxy. Although, maybe she's transferred all that to Norman now that she's married. At any rate, I know she's had to take steps to keep her son from taking over her life.

"You know I'm always here for you," I told her.

"I do know that. And . . . thank you, Lill."

"My pleasure." I could tell she was struggling to work up to telling me whatever it was she needed to say, so I reached for my cup and took a sip, watching as she pulled in a breath and firmed her lips. Once she started speaking, I forgot all about tea.

It was an amazing story.

"So, why don't you call the FBI and turn the art over to them?" I asked when she finished.

"Norman has some concerns. Agatha placed us in a difficult position by mailing us the pictures, and since she sent everything by parcel post, we have no way to prove where they came from. You see, the return address was a post office box, and probably a fake one."

"So he thinks the authorities might suspect him of the theft?"

"Oh, I doubt that. Besides, according to Norman the statute of limitations has expired. But that doesn't mean the FBI won't be interested in how we ended up with the paintings. Right now, we're waiting to hear from a private investigator Norman knows in Indianapolis who's trying to get in touch with Agatha and Stanley."

"And in the meantime, you're going to distract yourself with a naked poker game," I said, taking a final sip of tea.

"Yes. And that's why I need your help. You see, Myrtle walked in right after the first batch of pictures arrived, and I was looking at one of them. I don't know how much she saw, but you know Myrtle. She commented that the picture seemed to be old and pushed me to open the other boxes, which she was assuming were wedding presents. I had a devil of a time distracting her. The only way I could get her to leave was to agree to the game. But I'm afraid she'll bring it up again and ask me what was in the packages. So I need your help to keep her curiosity contained."

It was a measure of how unsettled Josephine must be that she would feel the need to ask my advice about something this simple. "Let's see. The boxes were rectangular, you say?"

"And flat. But there were two tubes as well."

"So . . . why don't you tell her they were just some fixtures. I know . . . how about curtain rods."

"And the picture?"

"What'd she see?"

"Only the edges, I hope. It was a da Vinci drawing of a man on a horse."

"Hmm. Okay, maybe it's . . . an old map. And you bought it as a present for Norman."

"So Norman is a fan of old maps?"

I gave her a bland look. "Who knew?"

With our plans successfully hatched, Josephine's shoulders relaxed, and her frown lines smoothed.

# Chapter Seven

## *Josephine*

Myrtle doesn't have enough room in her apartment for more than one guest, given it's stuffed with gimcracks and furniture that should be put on a diet, so we met for our game in the library.

When Lill and I arrived, Myrtle was sitting at the round table in the corner, chatting with a man and a woman. The two stood to greet Lill and me. If they were a couple, they were an unlikely one. A Mutt and Jeff, although the woman was the tall one. Compared to her, the man, who was short, had an unusually delicate bone structure.

"These are the Mekyles," Myrtle trilled. "Malcolm and Thelma. They just moved into your old apartment, Josephine."

"Good to meet you," the woman said in a robust voice that fit her rangy physique.

Malcolm's voice, surprisingly, was equally robust, one of those that can be heard clearly even when he's across the room whispering into someone's ear. I tried to remember where else I'd heard the name Malcolm recently, but the memory proved elusive.

"Malcolm was an actor," Myrtle said. "On Broadway. And Thelma . . . what is it you said you did?"

"I was a dresser."

"Of course." Myrtle obviously didn't have a clue what a dresser was, and was running possibilities through her mind. One image she was no doubt struggling with was that of the six-drawer dark oak monstrosity adorning her bedroom that I glimpsed the one time I'd been in her apartment.

"Is that how the two of you met?" I asked. "On Broadway?"

Thelma smiled, and when she did, I could see what had attracted the diminutive Malcolm to her. "As a matter of fact, it was."

Myrtle was still obviously struggling for a synonym for dresser, which, unfortunately for her, didn't exist. "How nice," she said, motioning for all of us to take our seats, and making it clear the subject of Thelma's choice of career was off the table.

I exchanged a look with Thelma, deciding that maybe the afternoon wouldn't be as awful as I'd anticipated.

As Myrtle dealt cards for the first hand, Malcolm turned to me. "I understand you used to have our apartment. Did you have to put up with that parrot? Every time Thelma steps out, it screeches 'penis' at her."

Thelma nodded. "It's horribly unnerving."

The parrot, with whom I was well acquainted, usually only said its word when a man came into view. Glancing at Thelma, I could understand what had confused the parrot. However, it would be unkind to share the bird's usual gender-specific propensities.

"It doesn't seem to like tall people. It yelled at all our tall visitors until the manager decided enough was enough and exiled it to a less public location."

"You could ask for it to be moved." Lill's brows raised, but she kept mum about the parrot's usual targets.

"It just hates men." Myrtle humphed, clearly oblivious to our attempts to mask the parrot's true proclivities. "It learned everything it knows from Pru Parker. Every man in the place picks up his pace when Pru appears. As a matter of fact, I've never heard another woman ever complain about either Pru or the parrot."

Thelma's face turned pink. "Oh."

I turned toward her. "When it was first moved outside my door, it yelled at me all the time. I just covered it up until it mended its ways."

Myrtle's eyes widened. "You never told us that."

"It yelled at me too," Lill said, backing up my lie.

Myrtle sniffed. "Well, aren't you two as thick as thieves. So, who needs cards?"

It wasn't until the fifth hand that Myrtle mentioned the boxes she'd seen on my table.

"So . . . what was in the packages, Josephine?"

I glanced up from my cards, my pulse rate going up. "Packages?" I concentrated on keeping my hands, which were gripping my cards, from trembling.

"Yes. The ones that had just arrived when I came to see you the other day. Were they wedding presents?"

I shook my head and tossed a couple more paper clips into the pot. "Nothing so exciting. They were curtain rods."

Myrtle sat back, her lips in a skeptical curl. "If they were curtain rods, where were the shipping labels?"

"I have no idea what you're talking about."

"They were addressed by hand. I saw that much. What company addresses shipments by hand anymore? Even I know computers do everything these days."

"Really, Myrtle. I have no memory of how they were addressed. All I can tell you, boring as it may be, is that they were curtain rods."

Lill slid two paper clips into the pot. "Isn't it about time to see who has to tell a story?"

I shot her a grateful look for the deflection.

"Well, that picture you were looking at for sure had nothing to do with curtain rods," Myrtle said, undeterred from her bone.

"Of course not. It was a copy of an old map. I bought it as a gift for Norman."

Malcolm gave me an eager smile. "Your husband's an admirer of old maps?"

"He does seem to like them." I smiled back at Malcolm and hoped my noncommittal answer would be sufficient. I was beginning to feel like I was surrounded by a pack of dogs nipping at me. I sent Lill a pleading look.

"We're getting off the subject here." Lill glanced at Myrtle. "I think Myrtle's just trying to get out of telling a story, because she's our biggest loser."

Myrtle's mouth opened and shut like a fish gasping, and she glared at Lill. "Indeed. I am not the biggest loser. Malcolm is." She sat back, crossed her arms, and nodded at Malcolm.

"I'm sorry." Thelma laid down her cards. "I thought this was just a friendly game and that the stakes were paper clips."

"Myrtle didn't tell you?" Lill said. "We play for stories. The biggest loser has to tell something good and juicy. And true, of course. We've had stories from both a thief and a murderer. So you can see our standards are quite high."

"My best stories are held under the seal of confession," Malcolm said.

Myrtle sat up with a clatter. "You're a priest? Aren't you and Thelma married?"

Thelma frowned. "Of course we are. What Malcolm means is that he never betrays a confidence. Just like a priest."

Lill chortled. "Only different."

"If Malcolm declines to tell a story, I can be magnanimous and tell one instead," Myrtle said, reversing her earlier position.

Myrtle consistently manages to live up to the inspiration she provided for Lill to dub Brookside as Babbling Brook. Her stories might have been mildly interesting the first time we heard them, but Lill and I are into the fourth or fifth retelling, and they're not improving.

Malcolm raised a hand in the air. "No, no, that's all right. I always pay my debts. However, I request a count to verify that I am indeed the loser." He pushed his small number of clips in my direction. "Perhaps Josephine could count mine, and I'll count hers."

I glanced down at my pile of clips to see that it appeared smaller than it had moments before. And, indeed, when the count was done, the conclusion was that I was down one clip compared to Malcolm, who sat back with a satisfied smirk. Myrtle was third. I had no doubt that Malcolm had poached my clips. From right under my nose.

"Well, Josephine. Looks like you're our storyteller today." Myrtle added her smirk to Malcolm's.

I hate being put on the spot. It was most aggravating. Besides, I was positive I'd had one more clip than Malcolm. Which meant he'd removed two clips. One to add to his pile . . . and did he hide a second?

I glanced at the floor and noticed a clip lying there between Malcolm and me. I bent and picked it up.

"Here it is. I thought I had another clip." I held it up. "That means there's a tie." I'd decided I wouldn't accuse him of malfeasance; I'd just not forget what he'd done.

"But that's never happened before," Myrtle said. "What do we do now?"

"Since I'm the game's creator, I propose we both tell stories. I'll go first, and Malcolm second."

When I gave Malcolm a steady look as I said that last bit, he looked away and cleared his throat. "Yes. Of course. Whatever you suggest." Which told me I was right that he'd fiddled with my clips.

I'd decided to accept a tie because I'd figured out I could tell the story about Norman suspecting I was one of the Elizabeth Kent Oakes robbers. After all, it does have a rather satisfying ending.

I was only a short way into the narrative when Myrtle interrupted to correct a detail. "You can't be so loosey-goosey with the facts, Josephine."

Irritated, I continued.

She interrupted again. "That wasn't what happened."

I sat back. "Why don't you go ahead, Myrtle? You seem to know what happened to me better than I do."

"It's your story, Josephine."

"Not with you constantly interrupting." I muttered under my breath, knowing she couldn't hear me since she wasn't wearing her hearing aids. But even with them in, Myrtle tends to mishear and misinterpret events, leading to skewed reports of even simple happenings.

I picked up the thread of what I'd been saying and tied up the ends quickly before Myrtle could interject any more comments. Although, perhaps her obvious misstatements served to throw a pall of uncertainty over her report of sighting mysterious packages on my dining room table.

Finished, I turned to Malcolm. He bowed his head, but when he straightened, his expression was calculating.

"We don't bite, you know," Lill told him.

"But we do have high standards." Myrtle began gathering paper clips and cards. "Just remember, thief and murderer."

"I can't possibly top that. I've led a very boring life, overall."

"Everyone has at least one skeleton, literal or figurative, in their closet," Lill said.

Myrtle let out a satisfied humph. "Yes. Everyone."

"Well, how about—"

"No." Thelma's tone was both definite and admonitory. "You can't tell that one."

"What can I tell, then?"

"You were an actor," Myrtle said. "If you don't have a juicy personal story, surely you can dish some dirt on someone you worked with. Someone famous, of course."

Malcolm's mouth did some odd twisting and grimacing. Finally, it firmed. "Well, yes. I could do that. As a matter of fact, I believe I know the perfect story."

Thelma was watching him intently. As if warning him about something, was my interpretation.

"First of all, you have to understand this happened a few years ago," he nodded at Myrtle. "To someone famous, although I didn't know him well. But a friend told me about it, and it was such an intriguing story, I've never forgotten it."

"You have to tell us his name," Myrtle said.

"Jonathan Jones."

Myrtle frowned. "I've never heard of him."

"He's the friend who told me the story."

"But it's not fair if you don't tell us the famous person's name."

"Seal of confession," Malcolm said. "The friend who told me about it insisted."

"So it's a story about someone that someone else told you?" Lill asked.

"Correct."

"But we want a *personal* story." Myrtle turned to me. "Don't you agree, Josephine?"

"You did say I could tell you a story about someone else."

"But this is what? Thirdhand? I don't know if that's acceptable," Myrtle said.

"Oh, for Pete's sake, Malcolm. We don't have to do this. I say we leave."

Malcolm grasped Thelma's arm, forcing her to remain seated. "Let's not forget how much we want to fit in and make friends here, my dear."

Thelma grimaced. "Of course. I'm sorry. You're right. And this is just a game, after all."

"Indeed, it is." Myrtle lifted her chin. "But one we take very seriously."

It was a statement that clearly didn't reassure Thelma. She bent and whispered in Malcolm's ear. My guess was that she told him to make something up. If he wasn't already planning that. But I could be wrong.

"Now, Malcolm," Myrtle said with a trill. "Do please continue."

"Yes, okay. Where was I?"

"A friend told you a story you've never forgotten," Lill said. She never loses the plot.

"Ah, yes. This man, he was a leading man, you see. Very strong, very masculine. He fell in love with an actress he met while making a movie. She was beautiful, and he . . . lost his head. Divorced his wife—luckily, there were no children—and asked the actress to marry him. Then, on the honeymoon, he discovered that she was a he."

"Pish posh. I don't believe it," Myrtle said. "Young people these days have sex at the drop of a hat. He would have known after the first date."

That made Lill and me blink at each other. And it brought to mind the unwelcome image of Myrtle and Bertie locked in an amorous clinch. Bertie has now moved on, but still.

"This was back when premarital sex wasn't so common," Malcolm said, and Thelma snorted. "The actress . . . she said she wanted to wait for their wedding night."

"But they were actors," Myrtle said. "I've read movie magazines for years. I don't believe a word of it."

"What happened when he discovered she was a he?" Lill cocked her head so her good ear was turned toward Malcolm.

"Why, they lived happily ever after," Malcolm said, his Adam's apple bobbing.

*Sure, they did.* It was a thought I kept to myself. Because while everyone was focused on Malcolm, I'd switched my attention to Thelma. She had a hand to her throat, looking very upset. And it all clicked into place.

This wasn't a story about some anonymous actor and actress—it was Malcolm and Thelma's story. Modified, of course. And if I were any judge, there was an excellent reason Thelma always wore scarves. Further, it was clear the parrot had been much more observant than we had been.

"And that's it. That's the story?" Myrtle said. "Well, I don't think it counts."

"It's fine," I said, losing patience. "Besides, it's almost dinnertime."

I looked pointedly at my watch. Thelma's shoulders visibly sagged. Lill raised an eyebrow with a slight twist of her chin toward Thelma, and I nodded.

Myrtle, missing all the byplay, struggled to her feet. "I believe you're absolutely correct, Josephine. It is almost time for dinner."

And if there's one event at Brookside that Myrtle has no intention of ever missing, it's a meal.

~ ~ ~

"It was a most peculiar afternoon," I told Norman later. "Not only is Myrtle losing it, the new people were a couple of odd ducks."

After I described the events fully, Norman chuckled. "It sounds like Myrtle is still sharp enough to give you palpitations, love."

I shook my head, stepping in close as he put his arms around me. "I suppose you're right. That bit about the handwritten labels threw me."

"And she was right. That would be unusual if a company were sending you . . . curtain rods, you say?"

"That was the best explanation I could come up with in the heat of the moment." I didn't want to admit that Lill and I had brainstormed ahead of time.

"I'm not saying it wasn't a decent comeback. I'm just saying it proves Myrtle is still sharp enough to be a menace."

"I think you have a soft spot for Myrtle," I told him, leaning back.

"Of course I do. She's a grand old gal."

I gave him a look.

"But she's not my old gal." As the words left his mouth, I saw him realize what he'd said. His lips twisted. "One grand old gal at a time, I always say." Then he swooped in for a kiss that left us both chuckling and neither of us feeling old.

One of the things I like about Norman is that he makes me laugh. And the kisses are a bonus.

"Have you decided how to handle the paintings yet?" I hated putting an end to a playful moment, but the paintings were weighing on me.

"I have."

"Plan to share?"

He stepped closer once again and put his hands on my shoulders. "We need to have a meeting. I'd like you to invite Lill, Mac, and Devi. I'll invite Miriam O'Pinsky."

Miriam is the director of the Cincinnati Art Museum. Her inclusion, along with Mac's, meant Norman was going to transfer the paintings to the appropriate authorities.

It will be a relief to hand them over to someone else. After almost losing *Sea Watchers*, I don't feel comfortable having a stash of priceless paintings in my closet.

# Chapter Eight

## *Edna*

At dinner, Myrtle came bustling over to my table and plopped into the seat across from me. "Phew! That was quite a game we had today."

"Game?"

"I facilitated Josephine's introduction to that new couple who moved into her old apartment." Myrtle does crossword puzzles and loves to flaunt the ten-dollar words she discovers like *facilitated*, if she happens to remember them. "You know, the Mackinacs?"

It took me a second to translate. "Isn't their name Mekyle?"

"Pish posh. Does it matter? Anyway, Josephine lost, and she was not happy, let me tell you."

As one who has been present when Josephine lost at naked poker, I'm well aware of her dislike for losing. Although it's my theory her negative reactions have more to do with her dislike of sharing personal details of her life than the fact she doesn't like losing in general.

"But then she found a clip on the floor, which meant she was in a deadfall with Malcolm," Myrtle said.

"Deadfall?"

"You know . . . when there's a tie."

"Oh, you mean a dead heat."

"Yes, yes. So Josephine suggested they both tell stories."

"I'm surprised you got her to play."

"One just has to figure out the correct button to push."

Myrtle elevated her nose and gave me one of her superior looks. I'm quite certain she has no idea it makes her look like a poodle. A snooty one. And, of course, I am not going to be the one to tell her.

"And then, once she finagled the tie, Malcolm told a most peculiar story. And it wasn't even his story, which is strictly against the rules, as far as I'm concerned. But Josephine was the one who told a whopper. And I'm not talking about hamburgers."

I was having difficulty following Myrtle's stream of consciousness. "A whopper?"

"Curtain rods."

I barely stopped myself from rolling my eyes. "Curtain rods?"

Myrtle's attention had momentarily drifted to a nearby table, where Bertie was sitting with his newest conquest. He used to be Myrtle's gentleman friend, until she took him for granted one time too many, and his attention wandered.

"And?" I said.

She shook her head and shifted her focus back to me. "I was sure the boxes were wedding presents, and I wanted Josephine to open them, so I could see what they were. She refused. I was extremely annoyed with her. Then today when I asked her about them, she claimed the boxes contained curtain rods, and I know that can't possibly be right."

"Why not?"

"They were the wrong size, for one thing." She stopped and frowned.

"So, what do you think was in the boxes?"

"That picture that Josephine tried to hide had to be in one of them. The whole thing was extremely odd, that's all I'm saying."

The waitress showed up to take our orders, after which Myrtle went into a detailed description of the Mekyles. "They're quite peculiar. Even the parrot is confused. He thinks she's a he." She gave me a conspiratorial nod of satisfaction.

While I've never been impressed by Myrtle's powers of deduction, I am impressed by her recall of actual events, so I filed away the information about Josephine and the peculiar packages in my "mysteries to be explained" category. Recognizing and then investigating such inconsistencies are one of the few ways I have to add interest to my life.

I'm sometimes sorry I had to give up stealing. It kept my brain engaged . . . identifying possible targets, removing the items, and then making arrangements to turn them into cash with no one the wiser. It was good fun, actually. Until it wasn't.

I miss it.

But I'm a different person now.

I'm now a person who reads stories to small children as part of my community service sentence, and I'm delighted when one of them gives me a hug afterward.

~ ~ ~

Because I'm trying to be a better person, I gave Josephine a call to tell her about the conversation with Myrtle.

"Oh, fudge."

Josephine rarely curses, so I knew she was very annoyed.

"What's the matter?" I asked.

There was a pause before Josephine answered. "She's creating a mountain out of a molehill." She blew out a breath. "Okay. Here's the thing. Those packages didn't contain curtain rods, but I can't share what was in them. And the more Myrtle keeps gossiping about them . . . it could cause a major problem for me. And for Norman. So anything you can do to deflect her would be hugely appreciated."

I was now as intrigued by the boxes as Myrtle appeared to be. However, I assured Josephine that I'd do my best to change the subject if I heard Myrtle mention them again.

"I promise to tell you what's going on when I can, but meanwhile, I appreciate the help."

"That's what friends do," I said. "They help each other."

"Of course. Thank you, Edna."

I hung up smiling. Not only had Josephine trusted me with information she wasn't sharing with Myrtle, she'd called me a friend. Or, at least she hadn't contradicted me when I called myself her friend.

# Chapter Nine

## *Lillian*

I was so pleased to be included in the meeting where Josephine and Norman would be revealing that eight works of art, worth more than several small countries and the state of Mississippi, had been mailed to them by an unknown entity.

*Unknown entity* was how Josephine referred to the couple they'd met in Indianapolis. "After all, we don't *really* know for sure who mailed the paintings," was her excuse.

Regardless of how the art arrived and from where, my being included in the revelation meeting was exciting. In preparation, I visited the beauty shop, something I rarely do, and I wore one of my best church dresses.

Looking at myself in a mirror, I decided something was missing. And then it hit me. The dress needed a hat to set it off. I returned to my bedroom and carefully lifted the navy-blue large-brimmed hat with its feathers and flowers off the shelf and settled it on my head.

*Mm-hmm, do I look good.*

Devi picked me up and drove the short distance to Josephine and Norman's new home, saying that Mac would be arriving separately.

"Do you know what this is all about?" Devi asked.

"I have a suspicion. Indeed I do," I told her.

"Care to share?"

"Now, child, I don't want to ruin Josephine's surprise."

Luckily, we'd arrived at that point, and there was no time for more questions.

Mac waited at the curb for us. "Nice hat." He offered me a hand to climb out of Devi's car, and I gratefully accepted.

"Hardly," Devi said. "It's an amazing hat."

"Yes," I said. "It is, isn't it."

"From the way you're dressed, this must be a really important meeting," Mac said.

"Mm-hmm. You have no idea." I gave him my mysterious smile. Then I did that thing with my lips that Myrtle does, like I'm zipping them. This was the only situation I'd ever felt like it was a remotely appropriate thing to do.

Devi gave me a skeptical look. "You sure seem to be enjoying yourself."

"Oh, indeed I am."

Mac offered one arm to me and the other to Devi, and the three of us proceeded to Josephine's front door as if we were walking down the aisle at Westminster Cathedral.

Josephine opened the door, gave my hat an envious look, then ushered us in. I confess I've gotten out of the habit of wearing hats since my Roger died, but given the response so far, I might want to rethink that.

We took seats in the living room, and I noticed immediately that the coffee table sported an upside-down paper box lid. I made a bet with myself about what it concealed.

"We're just waiting for one other person, and then we'll get started," Josephine said. "Tea, anyone?"

We all declined. I, at least, was too interested in what was going on to juggle a teacup. Besides, if we were going to see what I thought we were, there shouldn't be any liquids in the vicinity.

The doorbell rang, and Josephine disappeared briefly, reappearing with Miriam O'Pinsky. I watched Mac and Devi, and noticed Mac's surprise morph into something approaching satisfaction. I wondered how he could possibly know about the paintings. But then, he is a rather surprising man.

Since we all knew Miriam, brief greetings sufficed. We settled, and Norman stood and thanked us for coming.

"Jo and I are dealing with a dilemma, and we're grateful we have such good friends to help us resolve it." His hand rested on Josephine's shoulder, and he glanced at her before continuing. "On Wednesday, four packages were delivered to us by the post office. A day later, four more arrived. The labels were handwritten, and the return address was not the origin of the packages. Something we checked after we saw the contents."

Again, he stopped and glanced at Josephine, who reached up and gave his hand a squeeze. "We opened one of them and found this." Norman lifted the box lid off the coffee table. Underneath, as I expected, was a drawing of a man on a muscular horse. Both the ink and the paper had the golden tint of extreme age.

There was a collective gasp. Or perhaps it was only Devi and Miriam who gasped.

When I'd first heard about the Elizabeth Kent Oakes heist, after Josephine and I discovered Norman suspected her of being part of it, I'd gone to the library and checked out several books on art theft. They all mentioned that particular theft, and several included photographs of the missing paintings and drawings. And this was one of them. It had last been seen hanging in the Elizabeth Kent Oakes Museum in Boston forty-three years ago.

Miriam leaned over and peered at the drawing. "You're saying someone mailed you a priceless da Vinci drawing?"

"Yes. All the packages arrived by regular first-class mail."

"And they contained the artworks stolen from the museum?"

"Yes. We opened the packages but handled the contents only enough to identify them. All the missing artwork appears to be here."

"This is . . . Wow . . . I can't even find words," Miriam said. "The post office. Unbelievable." She sat back. "You realize these need to be moved to a climate-controlled vault as soon as possible."

"Of course. That's why we invited you today."

"What about the rest of us?" I asked.

Norman nodded as if pleased to hear the question, but Josephine was the one who answered. "We invited the rest of you to serve as witnesses as we transfer the paintings and drawings to the Cincinnati Art Museum."

"We're doing this as an interim measure to ensure they're kept safe until the owner can be verified," Norman added.

"Isn't the owner the Elizabeth Kent Oakes Museum?" Miriam said.

"The museum has never released information on whether there was an insurance settlement," Norman said. "Our concern is that there may be competing ownership claims. That's why we feel a disinterested third party is the best place for the art to be held until that's sorted out."

"There's also the question of the crime itself," Mac said. "The art fraud division of the FBI is going to be very interested in this sudden reappearance, and in particular, the packaging that was used."

"You're right. And we hope that you'll contact them on our behalf."

"Does this have anything to do with your trip to Indianapolis?" Devi said. "The trip you said was a wild goose chase?" She gave both Josephine and Norman what I interpreted as a suspicious look.

Josephine hesitated before saying, "We're not free to discuss that at this time."

That surprised me. It seemed that Josephine had kept Devi in the dark, and Devi now knew it. I was sorry to see this rift, because the relationship Devi and Josephine share has been special to them both.

Norman kept his hand on Josephine's shoulder, but he addressed Devi. "Both Jo and I have given promises of confidentiality in order to ensure the safe return of the paintings. There are details about that return we're not free to tell you at this time." Then he included the rest of us in his glance. "Of course, the paintings will have to be authenticated."

"You mean they could be fakes?" The possibility shocked me.

"It isn't likely, but it is possible," Norman said. "And a good fake can be extremely difficult to detect."

I knew from my reading that art forgers are an inventive lot. One of the first things they do before copying a masterpiece is to get their hands on canvas woven during the time when the original painting was created. I think that's extremely clever. And they use the kind of pigments and paints used by the original artist, of course.

What with old paintings turning up regularly at estate sales and flea markets, all a forger would have to do is keep an eye out. Making something recently painted appear old would be trickier, of course.

I read about one forger who started as a restorer. As he worked with old masterpieces, he learned what he needed to know to create paintings that he passed off as lost masterpieces.

"I hope you'll be willing to accompany Miriam and the art to the museum?" Norman said, addressing Mac.

"Of course. I'll help any way I can," Mac said.

The drawing was carefully replaced in its tube, and we watched as all eight packages were transferred to Mac's vehicle. Then Mac and Miriam departed, in tandem, to the museum.

Norman put his arm around Josephine, and I detected sighs of relief from them both. Recalling what Norman had said about the FBI questioning their part in all this, I hoped their relief wasn't premature.

~ ~ ~

Since Josephine got married, I can no longer just walk down the Morning Glory-Mourning Dove hall and drop in on her for a cup of tea, and I miss it, and her. We no longer get to laugh together at the absurd bird/flower combination names anointing each of the halls in the main building. We shortened them for convenience. Ours, mine, is GloryDove. But there's also LarkLemon and our all-time favorite, SnapTit, which began life as Snapdragon-Titmouse. I've noticed residents of SnapTit all tend to mumble when you ask which wing they're in.

Although I miss Josephine, I don't begrudge her one iota of happiness. I just wish it didn't limit our chances of having new adventures, since our old adventures were so . . . invigorating—figuring out Edna was our Brookside thief, and even more spectacularly, discovering that Lottie Watkins murdered her aunt years ago and had never even been suspected, let alone caught. Our GloryDove days is how I appropriately think of them.

Now Josephine is involved in yet another adventure. But I'm not. The thought makes it hard to swallow, and I realize my eyes have teared up. I clench my hands into fists and take a breath. There's nothing to be gained from feeling sorry for myself. And Josephine did share the whole story about the paintings with me and no one else. Not even Devi.

I happen to know that Josephine considers Devi the daughter she never had, and Mac is a wonderful stand-in for Josephine's son, Jeff. All Jeff wants is Josephine's money. He even tried to have her committed in order to get his hands on it. Such a sadness for her. But I do believe she's safe now that she has both Mac and Norman watching out for her.

I set my disappointment firmly aside and headed to the dining room.

On the way, Edna caught up with me. "Can we talk, Lillian?"

We took seats at one of the smaller tables, and I laid my napkin on my lap, waiting for Edna to organize her thoughts.

"Have you spoken to Josephine lately?" she asked.

"Why, yes. I was at Josephine's and Norman's just yesterday." I smiled, proud to be one of only a half dozen people in the whole world privy to such a delicious secret. "Why do you ask?"

Before she could answer, Myrtle sailed over, grabbed a chair from another table, and joined us. "You two look cozy. What are you talking about?"

"I just asked Lillian if she'd seen Josephine lately."

"Good. I hooked you, didn't I." Myrtle gave Edna a nod and a look that oozed satisfaction that she then turned in my direction. "Curtain rods, indeed."

My heart sank. That again? Edna thinks Myrtle looks like a poodle, but I thought currently she was doing a darn good imitation of a pit bull.

"Curtain rods?" I echoed the words, playing for time.

"Why is Josephine lying about something silly like curtain rods? That's what I want to know." Myrtle sniffed. "You were there, Lillian. Did you believe her?"

"I had no reason not to." I chose my words carefully. I do try to be a good Christian woman, but sometimes one simply has to stretch the truth.

"You need to talk to her, Lillian. You're her friend. Find out what it's all about."

"Why do you care?" I said.

"Josephine isn't the only one who can investigate a mystery. And it's certainly a mystery why she's lying about those packages."

"What do you think they contained?" I said in an effort to deflect.

But Myrtle was on a roll. Unstoppable. "I know one of them contained a picture. A very old picture."

"A map, I believe she said."

Myrtle snorted.

"What did you see?" Edna asked, finally joining the conversation.

"It had uneven edges, and it was this sort of brownish color, and I could see part of a horse. Josephine was blocking the rest. But how many maps, even if they're very old, would have a horse on them? And I'm quite certain it was old." She stopped and put a finger to the corner of her mouth. "You know what I think?"

"I haven't the faintest idea." Then I wanted to kick myself for taking the bait.

Myrtle's satisfaction more than oozed; it practically rolled over me in a smothering wave. "I think it was an old picture. I mean, even I could tell that. I think it has something to do with whatever Norman is investigating. Yes. That's it. It was stolen art, mailed to Norman because he recovers things like that."

I swallowed. Who knew Myrtle was capable of spinning such an accurate conclusion out of such tentative strands of conjecture? "Norman's retired," was what I finally came up with in a vain attempt to steer her in a different direction.

"Nonsense. Once a detective, always a detective."

It would be fruitless to say Norman was an investigator, not a detective. Myrtle would probably say, "Pish posh." But if there's one way to distract Myrtle, it's with food, and luckily, our salads arrived at that moment.

Edna took a bite and gave Myrtle a direct look while she chewed. "That's a stretch, you know. Maybe she told you it was curtain rods because she was embarrassed by what the packages contained. You do realize she just got married. Maybe it was . . . I don't know . . . private stuff. Underwear. Sex toys, maybe?"

"Pish posh. You really expect me to believe that Josephine Bartlett would allow a sexy pair of underwear, not to mention a *sex toy,* anywhere near her body?"

"Maybe not. Maybe it was incontinence supplies for Norman." I was feeling desperate and trying to follow Edna's lead. But my suggestion seemed to gain some traction.

Myrtle frowned, then she shook her head. "Wrong kind of box. I'm quite certain I'm right. Those boxes were exactly what you'd use to mail stolen paintings."

"Oh, I doubt that," Edna said. "Who would *mail* valuable paintings? A lunatic, maybe."

"Well, I think it could be someone crazy as a fox," Myrtle said. "Hiding in plain sight. Anyone?"

"Why don't I ask Josephine?" I said. "Maybe she'll tell me, and then I can tell you."

Myrtle thought about that for a minute. "O . . . kay." She was obviously reluctant to give up control of her news. Like me, she doesn't have enough distractions in her life.

Edna remained silent, but I noticed she'd followed every word, and for whatever reason had tried to change Myrtle's focus. I was grateful for her help, and Josephine would be as well. But I did fear that if Edna's interest was snagged, she might be even more tenacious than Myrtle.

# Chapter Ten

## Mac

I didn't say it, but I knew this return could cause difficulties for all involved. The statute of limitations on the Elizabeth Kent Oakes heist may have expired long ago, but I knew the FBI was going to want any details about that heist and the art's return that Norman and Jo could provide. And then there was the breach of trust this return had caused between Devi and Jo.

Setting aside those worries, I followed Miriam to the museum, where I collected the packing materials after museum staff removed the art. Then I returned to the station and met with the chief to apprise him of the situation.

"You're absolutely positive this Norman Neuman wasn't involved in the original robbery?" was the chief's first question. He didn't include Josephine in his query, I assume because he knows who she is and has been impressed by her crime-solving skills.

"As sure as I am that you weren't involved," I told him.

"Hmm. He's the right age, though?" The chief had to be referring to the fact anyone involved in the heist would now be at least sixty years old.

"He is, but his entire career was spent tracking down lost and stolen art."

"He couldn't have a better cover, though. Steal the art, then return it for a reward. Makes for a nice diddle."

It was a good point, except, knowing Norman, I considered it impossible. But if the chief shared that theory with the FBI, they might not consider it improbable.

Although a moot point, the FBI might still pressure Norman about an alibi. So how difficult would it be for him to provide such an alibi for events that happened decades previously? If it were me, I'd be able to provide only generalities. For example, fifteen years ago I was a student at the University of Cincinnati, but I couldn't say for certain which classes I might have been taking without checking my transcript.

~ ~ ~

After the chief called the FBI, Agents Rosenberg and Collins showed up the next day. From their questions and comments, I knew they'd done their homework.

"Your chief says you'll vouch for the couple who claim the art was mailed to them," Rosenberg said.

"Yes, I know Norman Neuman and Josephine Bartlett, now Mrs. Neuman, well. I consider them both upstanding citizens. She's an art enthusiast, and she owns an Edward Hopper painting, but there's nothing in her background to suggest she's an art thief. And, as you probably know, Mr. Neuman spent his career recovering lost art."

"We understand she was living in Boston at the time of the Elizabeth Kent Oakes heist," Collins said.

"I believe that's correct." The internet. The not-a-secret keeper.

"That puts her in the frame." Rosenberg again.

"As for Norman Neuman, he's been involved in several high-profile recoveries. We agree with your chief that he could have been the thief." Collins. They were obviously used to interrogating as a team.

I hadn't been present when the chief called the FBI, but he'd obviously shared his theory. "You're saying the two of them stole the paintings, then laid low for over forty years before reconnecting and then returning the art? Seems an unusual scenario. And unlikely. Especially given what I know about them."

"That's a problem, Detective. Your relationship with these two individuals. We're going to have to ask you not to contact either of them until we conclude our investigation." Rosenberg.

"And how long do you anticipate that will take?"

"It takes as long as it takes." Rosenberg again.

"These paintings have an estimated value between two and three hundred million dollars. We don't intend to rush." Collins, with a smarmy smile.

"I thought they were valued at one hundred million?" Still an unimaginable amount of money.

"That was when they were stolen. They've appreciated in value since." Collins, still with the smarmy smile.

"So, who owns them now?"

"We'll take possession until that's determined. We're headed from here to the museum. Can you believe someone mailed these paintings?" Rosenberg huffed. "More likely this couple mailed the boxes to themselves and added the paintings after the fact."

The longer I spoke with Rosenberg and Collins, the lower my heart sank. The FBI didn't have a case, but they could still make life uncomfortable for Jo and Norman, and since I'd been warned off from contacting them, I wouldn't be able to help directly. Although, the agents obviously didn't realize they needed to also prohibit me from sharing my concerns with my wife.

Devi would consider that hairsplitting, and normally, I would as well. But not this time. Jo and Norman are family. As simple and complex as that.

As soon as the agents left, I called Devi, who was at the museum that day. "Can you take the rest of the day off?"

"Are the twins okay?"

"Yes. They're fine. But I need you to do something."

We agreed to meet at a café in Montgomery that was usually quiet that time of day, and I left the office as soon as I could. I didn't want to risk any further restrictions, and I needed to talk to Devi before Rosenberg and Collins figured out my wife's connection to Jo and Norman.

~ ~ ~

"Wow. I sure didn't see that coming," Devi said when I told her what the FBI agents suspected. "Since you can't talk to Josephine and Norman, I expect you want me to?"

"Would you?"

"Of course." She frowned.

"What is it? You're not still mad at Jo, are you?"

She shook her head. "I wasn't mad. I was . . ." Her shoulders lifted, and she gave me a wry smile. "Hurt, disappointed."

"Don't forget you're married to a police officer. I expect that's why Jo didn't tell you everything."

"You agree, though, that the trip to Indianapolis was probably connected to the art's return?"

"I suspect it was, given the postmarks on the packages."

Devi shook her head. "It's not good, is it?"

"It's probably going to be okay. They can't be charged with anything, but I'd like them to be warned what the FBI is thinking. The agents were heading to the museum to oversee the transfer of the paintings, so you may not have much time."

"I'm on my way." Devi picked up her purse and leaned across the table to give me a quick kiss.

Her reaction reassured me that Jo had been forgiven, and that my wife's sense of fair play was fully engaged.

## Chapter Eleven

*Devi*

I drove directly from talking to Mac to Brookside. With all the recent construction, a mix of houses, large and small, had joined the three-story main building that contained apartments. The entire community now covered at least twenty acres. Curving streets with bright white curbs connected everything, and grass and trees were slowly erasing the bare earth between the houses.

Josephine answered her door, took one look at me, and said, "What's wrong? Is Mac okay? Lily, Toby?"

"Everyone's fine. We need to talk. Is Norman here?"

"He's running an errand."

"Can you get hold of him and ask him to meet us at our house? As soon as possible? And then get your purse and come with me."

Josephine didn't hesitate or ask any questions, and within two minutes of my arrival, she was sitting beside me in the car. As we reached the Brookside entrance, a black Ford Explorer, the cliché federal law enforcement vehicle, turned in.

My heart sped up as I watched in my rearview mirror and saw it take the turn leading to Josephine and Norman's place.

"What is it?" Josephine said.

"It's just . . . that SUV. It looks ominous."

Josephine turned to look, but the SUV had already turned the corner.

"False alarm, maybe." I unclenched my hands and made a right turn out of the Brookside drive.

When we arrived at the house where Mac and I are house-sitting, I parked the car in the garage. The house has seven bedrooms, so I suppose it isn't surprising that it has a four-car garage. Norman arrived a couple of minutes after us, and I led the two of them into the smaller of the two family rooms in the main part of the house.

As the three of us settled in, Josephine relayed to Norman the basic information I'd given her on the way here about my conversation with Mac. "I knew they'd want to question us, but I wasn't expecting them to suspect us," she said.

Norman shrugged. "They have to consider every possibility. I've been questioned before when I returned missing art."

I considered that good news. "So, was this connected to your trip to Indianapolis?"

Josephine startled, and Norman looked grim.

Then he sighed. "Given the postmarks on the returned art, that trip is going to seem suspicious."

Josephine laid a hand on Norman's arm. "I have a confession to make. I . . . I told Lill the whole story. Afterward."

Norman smiled at her. "I'm not surprised. After all, Lill is both your friend and your partner in crime-solving."

I admit, it was another blow to know Josephine had confided in Lillian and hadn't also confided in me.

"It was an emergency. I needed help deflecting Myrtle," Josephine told Norman. Then she turned to me. "I didn't tell you any of it, Devi, because of Mac."

It was what Mac had already guessed, and I could choose to make a big deal of it, or I could accept her reasoning. I took a breath and went with the latter.

"Since we included you when we turned the paintings over to Miriam, the FBI may want to talk to you," Norman said. "That means it's best we don't tell you any more right now."

"Maybe you can ask Lill." Josephine looked first at me, then at Norman. "If she tells you what happened, it will all be hearsay."

"This isn't a trial," Norman said. "And during an investigation, the FBI will be happy to entertain hearsay." He turned to me. "If you know more, it could put you in an uncomfortable position. Better to wait until this concludes, and then we promise we'll tell you everything."

Although it didn't completely satisfy me, I could tell from Norman's tone and his expression it was all I was going to get.

I could also tell from the way Josephine was staring silently at her hands that she was as unhappy about the situation as I was.

# Chapter Twelve

## *Josephine*

After the meeting with Devi, Norman and I went home together. "Devi thinks she saw agents arriving as we drove out," I told him.

His hands tensed, then relaxed. "Probably better to get it over with sooner rather than later."

"Any advice?"

"Tell the truth, but answer only what they ask. And don't speculate or embellish."

Which sounded simple, but I doubted it would be.

By the time we pulled into our driveway, my mouth was dry, and I had a slight headache, despite Norman's reassurance we couldn't be charged with a crime. Two people sitting in a black SUV parked in front of our house climbed out and approached our front door. We walked in from the garage, and while Norman answered the front door, I went to the bedroom to comb my hair and put on my game face.

When I entered the living room, the two agents stood and introduced themselves. The large, intimidating one was Agent Rosenberg. He was accompanied by a small woman named Agent Collins who had limp hair and tired eyes.

After greeting them, it took considerable effort on my part to sit down and appear calm. But I was determined to follow Norman's advice, which boiled down to *don't speak unless spoken to.*

The agents seemed to be following a similar playbook. I was about to break the impasse by offering them something to drink, when Collins finally pulled out a notebook and pen, and Rosenberg cleared his throat.

"We're here to find out everything you know about the return of the art stolen from the Elizabeth Kent Oakes Museum on August seventeenth, nineteen seventy-four."

Until he mentioned the date, I'd had only a hazy recollection of exactly when in the 1970s the robbery took place.

Norman, with an interested expression, cocked his head at Rosenberg, and I firmed my lips to keep them closed.

"We'll be happy to answer your questions," Norman said.

I was pretty sure the expression I saw flicker across Rosenberg's face was annoyance. Which I found to be daunting, even if Norman didn't.

"How did the art arrive?" Rosenberg asked.

"It was delivered by our mailman."

"When did it arrive?"

"The first four packages arrived last Wednesday about two o'clock, and a second batch of four arrived the next day."

"Did you open them?"

The question seemed nonsensical to me. Of course we opened them. How else would we have known what was in them?

The questions continued in that vein for a time, and I let Norman handle them, only pitching in a word of agreement when Rosenberg specifically asked me to verify what Norman was saying. Throughout, Agent Collins took notes.

"Why did you turn the paintings over to Miriam O'Pinsky?"

That also seemed nonsensical.

"We wanted them to be secured in an appropriate environment as soon as possible."

"Why not call us instead?"

"I considered the museum was the best interim arrangement." Norman was obviously adhering to his own advice to answer only what was asked, and in the simplest possible way.

"Can you prove you didn't mail empty containers to yourself in order to make it appear that the art was returned by a third party?"

Norman didn't answer immediately, but I knew he wasn't surprised by the question. After all, Devi had warned us about this line of thinking.

"Actually, I don't believe I can prove that," he said finally.

Both Rosenberg and Collins appeared surprised by Norman's answer. As was I, frankly.

"Did you mail the packages to yourself?" Rosenberg asked.

"No, I did not."

"And you, Mrs. Neuman. Did you mail the packages in question?"

"No."

"You were living in Boston at the time of the original theft, I believe," Rosenberg said, keeping his attention on me.

I fought the urge to squirm. "Yes. I was."

"Were you involved in the theft? And please remember it's a crime to lie to the FBI."

"I was not," I said, although his mention of a crime made it difficult to swallow. But this ground was much firmer, and, after a moment, my heart rate, which had shot up, steadied.

"Can you prove it?"

"I believe I can. You said the theft took place on August seventeenth, nineteen seventy-four?"

"Correct."

"If the records haven't been destroyed, you'll find I was giving birth to my son that day." And who knew that I'd ever find my son providing me with such a key alibi after all the difficulties we have caused each other?

Collins scribbled madly, then glanced up briefly. "Which hospital?"

"Women's Lying In. In Boston."

She made a note.

"And you, sir? Can you account for your whereabouts on August seventeenth, nineteen seventy-four?" Rosenberg said.

"I'd have to check my records."

"Please do," Rosenberg said.

"Glad to," Norman said.

"So, why would someone mail the art to you?" Rosenberg looked at Norman with narrowed eyes.

"I don't know." Which, strictly speaking, was the truth. Just not the whole truth.

After a brief pause, Rosenberg stood, and Collins flipped her notebook closed. "We'll be examining the packaging," he said. "When that's completed, we may have more questions."

Norman simply nodded while I stiffened my spine to avoid sagging with relief.

# Chapter Thirteen

## *Mac*

Shortly after I arrived for work, the chief sent for me. He offered me a seat, which is usually a good sign. I was expecting the meeting to be about the investigation into Jo and Norman.

"I've been talking to the Loveland mayor. Privately." The chief tilted back in his chair. "They're very interested in your candidacy. How serious are you about the chief's position?"

I blinked to readjust my focus. "I haven't interviewed yet."

"Not answering the question."

"Until I interview and see the full parameters of the position, I won't know for sure."

"Full parameters, huh? But you're taking the interview. Has to mean you're well along in your thinking."

I'd overcome my surprise, and was back in the game, conversation-wise. "Yes, I am. Although I have serious reservations about giving up being a detective."

He nodded. "I remember having those reservations myself."

"How did you deal with them?"

"For the first three years, I took at least a shift a week in my old position as chief detective."

"Why did you stop?"

"Had to have a knee replacement back in eighty-nine. Couldn't manage the active stuff for a while. Started paying more attention to the admin side. Which I'd let slide, if I'm honest. Found when I didn't have the distraction of trying to be both the department's best cop as well as being in charge . . . let's just say, that's when I finally started to get a handle on this chief's job."

He stopped speaking, and I waited to see what he'd say next.

He sat forward, and the chair thumped down. "Being chief is demanding and interesting. A big responsibility. In my opinion, you'd be good at it. And if you're interested, you might consider staying right here."

This was an unexpected twist. I swallowed, wondering if my voice would work. "Here?"

"Not as young as I look. Wife's been after me to retire. Do some traveling. Before I do, I'd like to know I was leaving the department in good hands. Your hands."

I admit, his proposal was a curveball I wasn't expecting, and it took a moment to think of how to respond. Before I could, the chief continued.

"Already explored the possibility with the city manager. He and the council are behind the idea. Be happy to spend as much time as you need to get you up to speed, but I'd like to retire by next January. Don't expect it will take much to train you. And I'll always be at the other end of the phone, you need me. Anyway, it's your decision, but I'd appreciate you letting me know in the next couple of weeks."

~ ~ ~

Devi and I tried to put our worries about Jo and Norman out of our minds while we bathed and cuddled the twins before putting them to bed. I waited until we were in bed as well to tell Devi about my surprising meeting with the chief today, because having a coherent conversation when the twins are awake is pretty much a no-go.

I pulled her into my arms, and she spooned against me, which is my second-most favorite thing to do with Devi. "I talked to the chief today."

"Does the FBI still suspect Josephine and Norman stole the paintings?"

"Not sure. That wasn't why he wanted to see me." I paused, preparing to take the plunge. When Devi stilled, I spoke quickly. "He wanted to know how serious I am about becoming a chief of police."

"I thought you weren't telling him about that until you'd at least interviewed?"

"No. I let him know a while back."

The tension stiffening her body lessened. I continued to hold her.

"He asked if I'd be interested in the chief's job here in Montgomery."

She turned to look at me, and a couple of expressions chased each other across her face. Possibly the same expressions I'd had when the chief asked me that question.

"And you said?"

"He's given me two weeks to think about it. And to talk to you about it. So, what do you think?"

Her brow smoothed out. "Honestly, Mac? You didn't just jump up and down and say you were in?"

"I felt the situation called for a certain amount of decorum."

"And now?"

"I'm not much of a jumper. But, yeah, if you're good with it?"

She threw herself back into my arms, and that ended the discussion phase better than I could have hoped.

In reality, I didn't want to leave Montgomery. Even though Loveland is right next door, Montgomery is home. The place where I fit best.

## Chapter Fourteen

*Josephine*

"Mother, what the f—"

I held the phone away from my ear until the squawking coming from it slowed and then stopped. When I'd seen it was Jeff calling, I'd hesitated to answer. But it's sometimes better to get unpleasant things over with, and I had been expecting his call.

"Hello? Mother? Are you there?"

"Yes. Of course. But you know how much I dislike bad language."

"But the FBI, really? Did you steal that painting . . . the Hopper?"

"You mean the one I've given to the museum? Of course not."

"But you stole something."

"Is that what you told the agents?"

"I told them you seem to involve yourself with peculiar people, some of whom are criminals."

Which was true, I suppose. "How very helpful of you." I kept my tone pleasant, even though I felt like I was chewing a mouthful of nails.

"I'm your only family, Mother. I need to know when you're in trouble."

"But I'm married now, Jeff. So Norman is my family. And my next of kin. And I'm not in trouble." Which, strictly speaking, wasn't completely true. But if Jeff saw even the tiniest opening, he'd go for it guns, and court orders, blazing. Thank God I now have both Norman and Mac to watch over me. "Is there anything else you'd like to say to me, because I'm really very busy."

"Just, just . . . you must have done something. The FBI doesn't get involved in petty theft."

"Of course they don't. And it is a serious case. But I did nothing wrong. I'm sorry they felt they needed to speak with you."

With that, I disconnected from the call and sank into a nearby chair, breathing slowly and carefully until I got my irritation under control.

~ ~ ~

The private investigator Norman had hired to check on Agatha and Stanley sent his initial report. He'd found the Scotts' house closed up and no sign that anyone had been there for some time. Only two neighbors were willing to talk to him, and neither could recall seeing any lights in the house for at least a month.

"It's been completely dark at night, according to the neighbor whose house backs up to the Scotts'. She's up several times a night with a new baby. According to her, the Scott house hasn't been dark at night that she could ever remember. Said it didn't seem to matter what time she looked over there. There were always lights blazing. The last month or so has been a puzzle."

Norman told the investigator to check hospitals and hospice facilities, as well as death notices for the Scotts.

A day later, we received an email with an attached link to the official death certificate for Stanley. Working from the death certificate, the investigator found the funeral home that handled Stanley's remains. He called to tell us the little additional information he'd obtained, and I listened in on the extension.

"Stanley was cremated, and there was no service. A friend of the family picked up the ashes on behalf of the widow."

"What about this family friend?" Norman asked.

"Gave his name as Leonardo D. Vincent."

"And let me guess. You've found no trace of him either."

"Right. I suspect it was an alias. The funeral home didn't check ID, since he presented them with a cashier's check to pay for the services, and a letter from Agatha designating him as acting for her. There was no reason to question his authority in the matter. Oh, and he had a British accent."

"And there was no visitation either?"

"No. I did, however, pick up one bit of intriguing information that I need to follow up. I finally connected with another neighbor, and she mentioned a girl was living, or used to live, with Agatha and Stanley."

"A girl? Like a servant, you mean?"

"Not exactly. This neighbor has lived across the street from the Scotts for over thirty years, but said she never saw much of them. Which I think is understandable, given all the houses in the area have large yards with hedges and trees to provide privacy. But she said she did occasionally notice a girl coming and going, at least up until the last year or so. The only problem is the neighbor is quite elderly, and her account was vague. She also said she'd seen a man coming and going."

"Leonardo D. Vincent?"

"Possibly. The woman assumed he was Agatha and Stanley's son and the girl their granddaughter. But there's no record of them having children."

After telling the investigator to keep checking on possible friends or family of the Scotts, Norman hung up and frowned at me. "So Stanley died, and Agatha's done a runner."

"What should we do about our promise not to tell on her and Stanley?"

"Even if we tell, there's no way to prove we ever met with them. You see, there's more."

I closed my eyes, taking a deep breath. This was beginning to sound very, very bad.

"The investigator emailed earlier to say the house is owned by a company based in the Caymans. And he was unable to trace any actual person associated with that company."

"So, here we are, the recipients of art worth hundreds of millions of dollars, and no way to prove where it came from," I said in summary. "Surely, the FBI no longer believes either of us had anything to do with the robbery?" I knew I was in the clear with Jeff's birth. Even without hospital records, his birth certificate and his FBI interview gave me an alibi.

Norman's records showed that he'd spent that week driving to Florida for a friend's wedding. Since he was the best man, his presence at the wedding had been verified.

"But we're the only lead the FBI has. They're going to be aggressive about following it."

And with that bit of cheer delivered, Norman returned to the den to do whatever he could, I suppose, to check further on Agatha.

# Chapter Fifteen

## *Lillian*

I like to walk. And at my age, it's essential to keep moving. But Josephine's new place is far enough from the main building where I live that I'd hate to walk all that way only to discover she was out. So I called first.

"I have a better idea," Josephine said. "Let me pick you up, and we'll go to lunch."

Thirty minutes later, she pulled up by the front door. Her car is a snappy neon-green number, and it always surprises me to see Josephine driving it, as she's quite conservative in other ways.

Once we were seated in the Korean restaurant she'd chosen, and with the waiter's help had ordered, I told her Myrtle's theory about the packages.

"Wow. That's amazing," Josephine said.

"Maybe Myrtle isn't as flighty as we thought."

"Her coming up with that theory might turn out to be a good thing, though," Josephine said, her tone pensive.

"Because?"

"Because it might help make the case that Norman and I didn't mail empty boxes to ourselves. Myrtle can verify that at least one of them had a picture in it, since she caught me looking at it. A drawing by Leonardo da Vinci. The one we showed you the day we turned the art over to Miriam."

"I bet she'd enjoy being interviewed by the FBI. You know how much Myrtle loves attention, no matter where it comes from."

"I do. And I really don't want to involve her. But she may be able to help tie up that end of things. Thankfully, the FBI now seems to accept that neither Norman nor I could have had anything to do with the actual robbery. But they're still suspicious of our story of how the paintings were returned."

"Who could have guessed that Myrtle might hold a piece of the puzzle and be able to help you out?" I said, clamping down on the little imp of envy whispering in my ear.

Josephine lifted an eyebrow. "Indeed."

# Chapter Sixteen

## Josephine

Forgetting to check caller ID, I answered the phone to find Thelma Mekyle on the line.

"Josephine, Malcolm and I would love to go to dinner with you and Norman sometime. We so enjoyed meeting you, and we'd love to meet your husband."

I was still annoyed at Malcolm for poaching my paper clips, and I didn't want to be stuck in a restaurant with the Mekyles for the length of a meal. "Well, our—"

"I know, I'll bet you're really busy. You have so many friends. But I told Malcolm he owed you an apology for what he did at the naked poker game."

"Oh? You mean for helping himself to two of my clips?"

"How clever of you to notice. Not everyone does. You see, Malcolm's an amateur magician, and sometimes he gets carried away. I've told him not everyone finds him amusing. Although, I have to admit, we both enjoyed your story."

The apology was graceful, and took the wind right out of my sails of indignation. But I still wasn't convinced I wanted to go to dinner.

"I know," Thelma said into the lengthening pause as I tried to come up with an excuse. "I have a better idea. Why don't we go out for lunch? Do you like Chinese food? I know a place that does an amazing lunch buffet."

I glanced at the calendar we keep by the phone. I didn't want to do this, but the only way out was to be rude. Since I married Norman, I've been trying, with his encouragement, to be less of a grump. "Our only free day is Thursday."

"Thursday, it is." Thelma jumped in so fast, I was convinced it wouldn't have mattered which day I picked, she would have said they were available.

I hung up, puzzled by the invitation and her aggressiveness. But, after all, Thelma and Malcolm were new to Brookside, so reaching out to make friends was a good strategy.

And it was only one lunch. Norman and I could manage that. But from now on, I'd make sure I checked caller ID before I answered the phone.

I'd turned down Thelma's offer to drive us to the restaurant, saying we were going to be arriving from another appointment. Not true, but I didn't want to be trapped by their decision of when to end our interaction.

"They sound like an interesting couple," Norman said when I told him about the invitation.

"An odd couple is more like it."

"With a name to match?"

"I don't think someone named Norman Neuman should be casting aspersions on someone named Malcolm Mekyle."

"At least a buffet will take less time than ordering." He'd obviously assessed my level of enthusiasm correctly. "Just tap my foot when you're ready to go, and I'll make our excuses."

That, in a nutshell, is one of the reasons I love Norman. Along with a great sense of humor, he's intuitive, at least when it comes to me. At first it disconcerted me, but now I've come to rely on it.

~ ~ ~

Malcolm stood as we approached the table where he and Thelma were already seated. "So glad you were able to make it."

After I introduced Norman and greetings were exchanged all around, we ordered a pot of tea, and then Thelma suggested we go through the buffet line. *Good.* Things were moving along briskly.

"I was fascinated by your naked poker story," Malcolm said as we set down our filled plates and reseated ourselves. "And you were an art investigator." He turned toward Norman. "I'd love to know more about that."

Norman hesitated, a shrimp halfway to his mouth. "What is it you'd like to know?"

"How about . . . what was your most interesting case?"

Norman ate the shrimp with a thoughtful look on his face. "I expect it was the case of the Red Madonna."

"Oh, do tell. It sounds fascinating," Thelma said.

I tried to decide if she was really interested or just playing a part. Actually, maybe both of them were acting. But to what end?

"I was contacted by a man who'd replaced an original painting in a South American museum with a copy."

From that brief description, I was pretty sure I knew which of his cases he was talking about, although the "Red Madonna" moniker was new.

"Why'd he contact you?"

"He switched the paintings as part of a dare. The museum didn't realize the original was gone, but they had subsequently made a change to their security procedures, so the man was unable to return the original."

"Why not just keep it?" Malcolm said.

I glanced at him, trying to determine if he was serious. He seemed to be.

"He was a prankster, not a thief."

"So, what did you do?" Thelma asked.

"I spoke on his behalf with the museum director, who found the idea that they'd been fooled by a forgery of their most prized work for over six months deeply embarrassing. He was only too happy to arrange for the paintings to be quietly switched back."

"What if the forger didn't actually steal the original?" Malcolm said. "Maybe he conned you into replacing the original with a forged copy."

"Now that's an interesting thought," Norman said, giving Malcolm a considering look.

I wondered if Malcolm's reactions to the stories were indicative of a weak character or a strong imagination.

"Of course, the museum insisted that both paintings be examined. The forger had used a modern canvas and paints on the copy, so it was a simple matter to determine that the painting he was returning was the original."

"Was he charged?"

"No. The museum didn't want the publicity."

And neither did the young man. Norman had acted as a go-between, allowing the man to keep his identity secret from the museum. An echo of our current situation.

"And you, Josephine." With a bright smile, Thelma turned in my direction, her words pulling my full attention back to the ongoing conversation. "We've heard some very interesting stories about your Edward Hopper painting."

"You both had such interesting careers. An actor and magician, and a dresser, you said? I'd love to hear how all that came about." Given our recent experiences, I was beginning to feel distinctly uneasy with the focus of the conversation being so firmly directed toward stolen art.

Thelma glanced at Malcolm before she looked back at me with a smile that didn't appear to be quite authentic. A forged smile. The thought amused me. Today, she was wearing a red-and-black patterned scarf around her neck.

"We sure can't claim to have caught any art thieves, can we, sweetie." She reached out and appeared to give Malcolm's leg a squeeze. Was she communicating something to him, or just being affectionate?

Norman jumped into the gap and asked Thelma and Malcolm if they were art enthusiasts, which firmly turned the conversation back to the topic of art. Although, I have to admit, Norman steered it well away from art theft and its recovery.

I left the table to refill my plate. I'd taken a very small amount the first time and wanted more, as the food really was quite good. When I returned to the table, Norman had maneuvered Malcolm into talking about his favorite Broadway role. I listened as I ate. Malcolm named a play by a playwright I'd never heard of.

"So, why that role?" Norman asked.

Malcolm took a moment to answer as he chewed a bite of egg roll. Then he wiped his mouth and looked at us. His expression was the same one he'd had right before he launched into his naked poker story. As I had then, I doubted his veracity.

"I always give my characters a dramatic background, as part of my preparation." He shrugged in a deprecating way he could barely manage. "Perhaps I liked Gaylord the best because of what I came up with for him."

"And that was?" I asked, interested despite the fact I was quite sure the Neumans and Mekyles were not going to become bosom buddies.

"I decided that while piloting a small plane, he crash-landed in a grove of tall trees. He survived the crash and managed to pull himself out of the plane, only to find he was eighty feet off the ground." Malcolm's tone grew more enthusiastic as his words painted an ever more fantastic vision. "With great difficulty and even greater trepidation, he climbed down, but it left him with a fear of flying and of heights."

"Was being afraid to fly or a fear of heights part of the play's plot?" Norman asked.

"Not directly. But there was a hint that Gaylord had a traumatic experience. I simply supplied the experience. In my imagination, of course."

"But giving a character such a dramatic background, and one the author of the play hadn't envisioned . . . couldn't that skew your interpretation of the entire work?" I asked.

"Psychological depth trumps everything, in my humble estimation," Malcolm said, his tone, in my humble estimation, pompous.

I wondered if the director had been pleased with Malcolm's initiative. Or had Malcolm been a pain to work with? I suspected the latter. It seemed to me there was, in addition to pomposity, a sly cast to his pronouncements. Certainly, there was no humility on display. Or maybe I was still viewing him negatively because he'd scarfed off with my paper clips.

Either way, I was ready to end the interaction. I tapped Norman on the foot.

He immediately made a point of looking at his watch. "I'm afraid we have another appointment. We'll have to continue this another time." He reached for our bill, which the waitress had dropped off when she seated us. "Thank you for inviting us."

"Yes," I said. "Thank you. And you're right, Thelma, this was a good choice."

As we spoke, Norman and I stood up. The men shook hands, and Thelma walked around the table and inflicted a hug on me. I'm not much of a hugger, especially with people I don't know well. Another check mark against the Mekyles . . . overfamiliarity.

"We'll have to do this again," Thelma said.

I left it to Norman to murmur something noncommittal. Then we made our escape, stopping only to pay our bill at the bar.

In the car, Norman turned to me. "So . . . dinner next time. Our treat?"

"You're joking, I hope."

"Yep. Thanks for negotiating this down to lunch."

"They sure were insistent about asking you questions."

"Well, I have had an adventurous life," Norman said with a twinkle. "You know, though, I don't believe he's an actor. He may have acted in a play or two, but I doubt he'd have been a casting director's dream with that loopy attitude."

"A nightmare, maybe. And don't you think he's too short to play someone named Gaylord?"

I'd made a point of remembering the play's title and author, and now I wrote them down in the notebook I carry in my purse. It might be interesting to see if there was such a play, perhaps as a first step in figuring out exactly who the Mekyles were.

I had a very odd feeling about them. As if all the time we were with them, they were playacting for our benefit. And why on earth that might be, I didn't have a clue.

# Chapter Seventeen

## Mac

When the chief called me in, I expected it was to further discuss my decision to be considered for the chief's position, and I was ready for whatever he had to say. Or so I thought.

He opened with, "Your friends are in a great deal of trouble."

"You mean Jo and Norman Neuman?"

"I do. Seems they've returned forgeries rather than originals."

My chest tightened. "Why would they do that?"

"There's a ten-million-dollar reward."

"But Jo has enough money, she's donated a painting worth forty million to the art museum. And she pays a grant for . . . for the person who organizes the lending of that painting to other museums." I'm not sure the chief knows that Jo pays Devi's salary, and now was definitely not the time to enlighten him.

"Some people never seem to have enough," was his response.

I couldn't believe what I was hearing. "You seriously think Jo and Norman are trying to perpetrate a fraud here?"

"It's what the FBI thinks fits the evidence."

"What's the evidence?"

"They turned in stolen paintings that appeared out of nowhere. What other explanation is there?"

"But forging a diverse group of paintings and drawings . . . is that even possible? Who'd have the skill for something like that?"

"Mr. Neuman has encountered many forgers and thieves in his day, don't you agree? Besides, only one of the paintings has been found to be a forgery. So far." He shuffled through the files on his desk, then handed me a piece of paper. The chief came to computers late in life and still doesn't trust them.

I glanced through the note to find the name of the work that had been forged: *Storm on the Sea of Galilee* by Rembrandt. "And the remaining works?"

"Initially thought to be genuine, although tests are being repeated now that this has been discovered. Agents Rosenberg and what's her name, Cooper?"

"Collins."

"Yes, Collins. They're on their way here to interview the Neumans, so I hope your friends have an explanation."

I excused myself as quickly as I could. Since I'd recently searched out the images of the missing Elizabeth Kent Oakes art online, I knew the estimated value of each of the paintings and drawings. *Storm on the Sea of Galilee* was worth more than the rest of the paintings and drawings combined. If a person were going to forge something, it was the best choice, especially if the original had also been sold to a collector for an obscene amount of money. The zeros in a transaction of that sort were as mind-boggling as one of those multi-state lottery payouts.

A number of aspects of this whole affair didn't make sense, though. If the thieves—definitely not Jo and Norman—wanted to return the art, which it appeared they did, why include a forged copy of the most famous and valuable of the works? Whoever they were, they weren't going to be eligible to receive the reward anyway, since they'd returned everything through the Neumans.

So, why return forgeries . . . or a forgery? The whole affair was a puzzle.

I was beginning to understand the FBI's suspicions. Although I didn't doubt Norman, I could see why they did. I called Devi and gave her the task of letting Norman and Jo know about the forgery.

# Chapter Eighteen

## *Josephine*

I hung up from speaking to Devi, shaking. And when I told Norman about the Rembrandt being a forgery, I suspect he felt as sick to his stomach as I did.

"Is there any more news from your investigator about Agatha or the mysterious girl?" I asked.

He shook his head. "They've both vanished without a trace."

My stomach lurched, something it had been doing on a regular basis lately. Appetite suppression tip: do something to make the FBI suspect you of a crime. Works like a charm.

"We have to tell the FBI everything," I said.

"Even though it makes us look like patsies?"

"Better a patsy than an art fraud suspect." I shook my head in frustration. "The FBI can't seriously think we're anything but patsies, can they?"

"There's a ten-million-dollar reward for the return of the paintings, Jo. For a small cut of that, we could have hired an excellent forger."

"Why would we, knowing the scrutiny the painting would undergo? Why not return the other originals and skip the Rembrandt? Besides, what excellent forger do you even know?"

He raised his eyebrows.

"Oh. I see. That young man who switched those paintings. The Red Madonna case?"

"He's no longer young, and he's probably much more skilled. Although he promised me he'd use his talents only for the good."

"But each of us has a different view of what 'the good' is at any given moment," I said, remembering the young man was from a poor South American country.

"True. Which is one more reason I'm not looking forward to talking to the FBI."

~ ~ ~

This time when we met with Rosenberg and Collins, Agent Collins not only took notes, she recorded the interview. As I had the first time, I let Norman do the talking, answering only when directly asked about something.

"That's a pretty unbelievable tale you're telling," Rosenberg said after Norman had described our meeting with Stanley and Agatha. "Unless we can verify it, you may be looking at some very serious charges."

I didn't let myself think about that last statement. Of course they'd be able to verify everything. The house was there, along with the basement gallery, possibly still stuffed with art. The Rembrandt might even be there.

Despite Rosenberg's ominous pronouncement, listening to Norman detail our involvement, I felt less weighed down. But after he'd seen the agents out, Norman sat down, rubbing his forehead.

"What's wrong?"

"We need to face the possibility they won't find Agatha. Our investigator is very good, and he can't find her. Besides which, the other art may all be removed from the house. And the fact remains that we can afford a forger now." His expression was gloomy. "I fear they'll still see us as being involved somehow."

I had a thought, one that brought with it a dollop of optimism. "We forgot to tell them we have a witness who saw the paintings arrive."

"Who?"

"Myrtle."

"Didn't you say she couldn't have seen much?"

"She saw enough to suspect the explanation I gave her was a crock. Which it was."

"I doubt the FBI would consider Myrtle entirely credible."

"It's worth a try, though. Don't you think?"

He stood and paced back and forth before stopping in front of me and giving me a hug. Then he sighed. "It can't hurt. And who knows, it might help."

# Chapter Nineteen

## *Myrtle*

I cannot begin to tell you how exciting it was to help the FBI in their inquiries. What a lucky day it was for me when I walked in on Josephine and those mysterious packages.

"Oh yes, indeed," I told the agent. "The mailman walked right up to Josephine's door with those boxes. I was a block away, but my eyesight is excellent."

"And when you arrived, you saw the packages close up?"

"I certainly did. All piled on the dining room table, they were. Josephine tried to convince me they contained curtain rods, but I knew that couldn't be right."

"And why was that, ma'am?"

"They had these really unprofessional labels."

"Unprofessional in what way?" asked the woman, who was taking all the notes, and isn't that just the way of the world?

"Like something written by an old person. You know, all wavery and squiggly."

The man frowned at me. "Squiggly?"

"Here, let me show you."

I motioned for the woman to hand over her notebook, which she did reluctantly. Taking her pen, I wrote *Mr. Norman Neuman* as illegibly as I could manage. It wasn't easy because

I've always had very fine handwriting. In fact, I had to jiggle the pen a bit to get it right, but I was reasonably satisfied with the result.

I handed the notebook back, and she let the man see it. He raised his eyebrows at her and nodded. Clearly, they could see I knew what I was talking about.

"And the picture? You said it was of a horse?"

I launched into a description. The man turned his phone toward me, showing me a drawing of a horse. The figure of the man riding it was less definite, having no face. I took the phone and moved my hand over the part of the picture I hadn't been able to see, trying to decide if it was the one Josephine had moved so quickly to hide from my view.

"Yes. I do believe this could be it. It was larger, of course." I handed the phone back, and once again, the two exchanged a look.

"That's very helpful, Mrs. Grabinowitz."

"Oh, I do love to be helpful," I said. "And I was right, wasn't I?"

"About?"

"That those packages held stolen art that was sent to Norman, because that's what he does. He finds stolen art."

Agent Rosenberg cleared his throat. "What an interesting . . . um . . . theory, Mrs. Grabinowitz."

"Oh, it's more than that. And I figured it all out before the FBI."

I was already planning who I'd tell about my interrogation first. Lillian, probably, since I don't believe the FBI would ever want to talk to her. Then Edna. And maybe the Mekyles, who have been so friendly since the naked poker game.

I almost clapped my hands, I was that excited.

## Chapter Twenty

### Lillian

I swear, that Myrtle is one busy person. She sailed into dinner this evening wearing a purple garment that made her look like an enormous eggplant and headed to my table, snagging Edna along the way.

When Myrtle arrived, she was practically panting. "Girls, have I got news for you." She swept into place, bits of purple dipping into my water glass.

I removed the damp fabric and signaled the girl who handles the water that I needed a fresh glass.

With little fanfare, Edna sat down at the third place. She looked quite smart this evening in a bright green blouse with black slacks. Working on improving her character by changing her handwriting has also seemingly improved her fashion sense. At one time, I wondered if she was color-blind. Although, had she been color-blind, I suppose one would have expected her to wear outlandish color combinations, not the shades of beige that used to be her wardrobe staple.

Myrtle tapped me on the arm to focus my attention, which I admit had drifted. But given her obvious satisfaction—it was making her jiggle—I winced at the thought of what she might have to say. It rarely bodes well when Myrtle's so satisfied about something she jiggles.

"You'll never guess what happened to me today." She paused briefly, presumably to give us a chance to guess. But not long enough for us to actually put that guess into words.

"The FBI interviewed me." She sat back, her hands over her heart and a "so there" expression on her face. It was the expression she got whenever she told one of her beauty-pageant stories, and I distrusted it implicitly.

"I told them all about those mysterious packages of Josephine's, and I shared my theory."

"Your theory?" Edna said.

I wondered if I looked as mesmerized as Edna did.

"Yes. That those packages contained stolen art."

"You told the FBI that?" I had trouble getting the words out. They sounded like I was choking on something. Felt like it too.

"They were very receptive. I think that's what they suspected too."

At that moment, Myrtle spotted the Mekyles. With a *toodle-oo* and a clattering wave of her hand, she summoned them to our table. Edna and I were forced to shuffle closer together to make room for Malcolm and Thelma. And, of course, we had to hear about the FBI interview all over again.

"Wow," Thelma said when Myrtle had finished. "That's amazing. But why would someone mail stolen art to the Neumans?"

Myrtle waved her hand. "Well, Norman recovers stolen art, doesn't he? So it makes perfect sense."

"But who sent them the art?" Malcolm asked.

"How would I know?" Myrtle said. "I have absolutely no contacts with art thieves." Then she caught Edna's glance and again waved a hand. "Except for one. But that hardly counts."

Thelma's eyes widened. "You know an art thief?"

"She means me," Edna said in an annoyed tone. "And I've already told you, Myrtle, at least a dozen times, I did not steal Josephine's painting. I just had somebody relocate it temporarily."

"Edna is still doing community service, you know," Myrtle said with a satisfied sniff.

I could take no more of this. "Edna has apologized and is paying for her crime, so it's ungracious of you to bring it up, Myrtle."

Myrtle sat back abruptly, as if I'd slapped her, which had been my backup plan if she didn't stop gossiping.

"Well, I never, Lillian Fitzel. That is . . . that is most ungracious of you. I did nothing wrong. Unlike Edna." Myrtle's nose pointed up, the snooty poodle on full display, an image Edna had planted in my mind.

I shook my head, stifling both a chuckle and an exasperated sigh.

After the meal ended, Edna and I walked out together, and I told her I was sorry that Myrtle kept dragging up the past.

"That's okay, Lillian. It's a good way to remind me of how far I've come. And it keeps me from feeling too satisfied about my progress."

"I'm glad you see it that way. There are times when I'd like to use one of Myrtle's scarves to gag her."

Edna laughed. "If you did that, not only couldn't she speak, she wouldn't be able to eat." She clapped a hand to her mouth. "Oh my, that wasn't very nice, was it."

"That's okay. I wasn't being very nice either."

We went our separate ways, and I called Josephine to tell her what Myrtle was claiming to have told the FBI.

"We know. It was helpful, actually. It ended any suspicion on the part of the FBI that we mailed empty boxes to ourselves."

"Fancy that. And here I was feeling quite annoyed with her. Not to mention irritated that she outed Edna to the Mekyles."

"Outed Edna?"

"Isn't that what you call it? She told them Edna was an art thief."

"Poor Edna. Just when everyone's forgotten her crimes, Myrtle dredges them back up."

"If we ever find Myrtle murdered, we'd have to suspect Edna," I said. "Although I think Edna has mellowed over the whole episode. She loves her community service assignment, and if the price she has to pay is Myrtle continuing to remind people of what she did . . . well, I think she's okay with it."

"Funny how that's all worked out," Josephine said, sounding thoughtful.

"Yes, your Hopper painting has been a true blessing for Edna," I said. "So the FBI is finished investigating?"

"Not exactly. They've checked our alibis for the original theft, so they don't believe Norman or I had anything to do with that, but there's been a major wrinkle. The Rembrandt was a forgery."

That left me speechless for a moment. "O . . . kay. What does that mean, exactly?"

"It means we're back to the FBI suspecting us, this time of arranging for the forgery in order to collect the reward."

"What makes them think you'd take a chance like that?"

"The reward is rather large. Ten million, as a matter of fact."

"Surely they can see how foolish it would be for you to do such a thing."

"Yes. We're hoping that's what they'll conclude," Josephine said. "It was, however, an excellent forgery, and Norman is acquainted with at least one excellent forger."

I brushed all that aside. I knew neither Josephine nor Norman would knowingly be involved in such a scheme. The bad guys in all this had to be the Scotts. "What about the other art?"

"It appears to be genuine."

"That's good."

"Yes. The museum will be happy. Did you know they left empty frames in place, waiting for the art to be returned?"

"So, now they'll have only one empty frame."

"Yes. But if they had their druthers, they'd probably give up all the rest to have that particular painting back."

"Well, you and Norman are just going to have to find it for them."

# Chapter Twenty-One

## *Maddie*

After Stanley died, the man who had helped care for him returned to England. At least, that's what Agatha told me. I'd been out of town most of the last six months of Stanley's life, working on a commission to clean an eighteenth-century painting, so I'd seen the man only briefly, and he'd never been inclined to chat. I couldn't even recall being told his name.

Now I was back in Indianapolis, starting a new commission, and with both Stanley and his caregiver gone, Agatha asked me to move back in with her. I was happy to do that, although I missed my condo.

One afternoon, I returned from running errands to find Agatha sitting in the conservatory, breathing very carefully, her face pale and sweaty. Although obviously in pain, she wouldn't let me call 9-1-1.

"It's nothing. My chest just hurts."

"You should be checked, and I'm not budging until you agree." I got my phone out and was dialing when she grabbed my wrist.

"No. No ambulance. If you insist, take me to that emergency clinic. I'll be fine."

I didn't like it one bit. My finger hovered over that third digit, ready to press it.

"Please, Maddie. Don't fuss. The clinic will be fine."

What could I do? I drove her there, very carefully. At the clinic, I helped her into her wheelchair, which made her gasp in pain. Then I pushed her inside, wishing there were more I could do for her. After taking one look at her, the person at the desk called for a nurse, who came and wheeled Agatha out of sight.

Thirty minutes later, the doctor came to speak with me.

"I have your mother's permission to share my findings with you. I noticed a rattling in her chest, so I ordered an X-ray. She has pneumonia, and she's in quite a bit of pain. She needs to be admitted to the hospital for further tests."

"Pneumonia?"

"Did she ever mention any symptoms to you? Coughing? Difficulty breathing?"

I shook my head, suddenly remembering how during our private remembrance of Stanley, it seemed like there were times when her breathing had been labored. I'd thought she was simply fighting off tears. Agatha hates to cry, but I know she misses Stanley.

"Can I see her?"

"Of course." He led me to the room where Agatha sat on the examination table, wearing one of those gappy gowns. She appeared so much smaller than she had just minutes before, and her breath was raspy. One hand held the gown closed while the other clenched the edge of the table. I knew she was in pain when she stopped fighting the idea of the hospital.

An ambulance was called, and I followed it. At the hospital, a pulmonary specialist examined her and ordered more testing.

The next day, he came to Agatha's room and faced us both with a grim expression. "In addition to pneumonia, Mrs. Scott, you have several tumors. We don't know what the primary is, but there's both lung and liver involvement."

"And treatment?" The words squeaked out of me. I glanced at Agatha, whose eyes had closed. She appeared to be serene, not at all like someone who'd just been given a terrible diagnosis.

"My advice is that you transfer your mother to hospice care. They'll be able to keep her comfortable."

"Hospice. You mean . . . she's going to . . ." I simply couldn't say the next word.

The doctor glanced at Agatha, who seemed to be sleeping. He nodded. "I'm afraid so."

"How long . . ."

"Not long. I'm sorry." We stared at each other, then he shifted uncomfortably and turned to leave.

The door had barely shut behind him when Agatha hit the button to raise her bed. "Thank goodness we got that over with. Poor man. He really needs to work on his bedside manner."

"You weren't sleeping?" It was a stupid thing to say, but Agatha looked and sounded so much like her usual self, the previous few minutes felt like a hallucination.

"When you have as little time left as I do, you can't afford to spend any of it sleeping. Now, go and find out what you need to do to get me out of here."

~ ~ ~

I managed to delay her leaving the hospital for three days, but when we left, it was still against medical advice.

Those three days had been busy ones. At Agatha's direction, I removed most of the art, all of my things, and Agatha's jewelry from the house, taking them to my condo. I left behind ten paintings Agatha said were to stay in the house.

I packed a suitcase for Agatha and another one for myself. Then I booked tickets for the two of us to fly to Denver, where I rented a car and drove to the MountainView Nursing Home. Agatha, anticipating that Stanley would die first, had done her homework on where she preferred to be when the end was inevitable.

"I need to see the mountains again." It was only then that she admitted she had been born in Denver, and that she acquired her English accent and her exotic name in her twenties, and then kept both when she found them useful in assuring her position in Indianapolis society.

Her room at MountainView did indeed overlook the mountains, but she didn't get to enjoy it for long. The effort to get her relocated had sapped her strength, and I doubt the high altitude helped. After a week, she required larger and larger doses of pain medication that left her drifting in and out of consciousness.

During what was her last bit of lucidity, she gripped my hands. "Maddie, you need to know, Stanley wasn't always a good man. But he changed because of you. He even helped . . ." She stopped, trying to catch her breath.

"Helped who? Do what?"

"The paintings . . . not . . ." She struggled to breathe, and my heart stuttered.

Without any warning, tears dripped down my cheeks, but I ignored them. The most important thing in that moment was to hold on to Agatha. To keep her with me.

As I stood over her, her eyes closed. She'd fallen asleep. I sat down near the bed, still holding one of her hands, waiting for her to wake up, beginning for the first time to accept that I'd be going back to Indianapolis alone.

While I waited, I wondered what words had been left unsaid. The paintings were not . . . what? And Stanley had helped . . . who?

Agatha died two days later without waking up, without adding to those words, while I dozed in a recliner next to her bed.

As she'd requested, she was cremated. She'd already told me before we left Indianapolis that I was to mix her ashes with Stanley's and then sprinkle them somewhere in the mountains. It was three days before I received her ashes, and I no longer have any memory of what I did, or who I saw during that time, with the exception of one conversation I had with Agatha's night nurse.

She was the one who gave me a suggestion for where to carry out Agatha's last wish. I hadn't told her it was to sprinkle ashes. I'd said only that I wanted to find a place in the mountains to hold a private remembrance. But I'm certain she suspected.

"Maybe Central City. It's an old silver-mining town, and it's quiet, peaceful, this time of year. There's a cemetery at the top of the main street."

I remember nothing of the drive to Central City, but I do remember finding the cemetery, right where the nurse said it would be, with its view of snow-covered mountains. I'd stood there after carefully sprinkling the ashes where they wouldn't be noticed. Words from a hundred movie funerals swirled around me. *The Lord is my Shepherd . . . may they rest in peace . . . the sure hope of resurrection . . . ashes to ashes, dust to dust.*

Neither Agatha nor Stanley belonged to an organized religion, and neither did I, and so the words were truncated, bits and pieces that I made no attempt to extend or to weave together. My own eulogies were wordless. Although I'd known, given Stanley and Agatha's ages, this day was coming, knowing and experiencing were two very different things.

I'd had little opportunity to grieve for Stanley, because his death had led to a flurry of activity carried out at Agatha's bidding, culminating with this final act. But now, saying goodbye to the only mother and father I'd known, in a town rendered silent by the onset of winter, grief doubled me over. They had been wonderful parents. Loving and caring. Supporting me and providing me with the skills that were shaping my life's path as an adult.

Agatha never baked chocolate chip cookies, but she taught me to accept myself by accepting and loving me. And Stanley may have never come to a parent-teacher conference, but he'd patiently helped me with homework, and he'd practiced lines with me the one time I had a part in a school play. And they had comforted me whenever my heart was hurting.

I will miss them both the rest of my life.

~ ~ ~

Before we'd left for Denver, Agatha told me I was not inheriting the house, which wasn't a hardship as I had no desire to live there. When I returned from Colorado, I met with the executor, who shared that the house was separate from the trust containing the rest of their assets for which I'd been named trustee. When he told me what the trust was worth, I gasped. There were sufficient assets to last my lifetime, even if I lived as many years as Agatha and Stanley had.

From what Agatha had said, I suspected the house might be left to gently molder, hopefully with little notice and over a period of years. Knowing about the art left behind in the basement gallery, I was relieved to know I had no further responsibility for it.

I further understood the reason I'd been instructed not to return to the house after I examined the paintings Agatha had directed me to remove from the house. I discovered that all were listed in databases as having been stolen. The difficulty, and the possible danger, was that Agatha didn't know which of the paintings were originals and which were forgeries Stanley had painted.

My guess about what Stanley did with his copies had been only partially correct. Rather than exhibiting the fakes in order to spare the originals, he'd sold them, although Agatha was uncertain if in every case Stanley sold the copies. It meant the paintings in my closet could be a mix of priceless masterpieces and worthless copies. But if they were the real deal, and word got out they'd been returned to the owners they'd been stolen from, unhappy collectors owning the copies might come seeking refunds or revenge.

Agatha had left me with a conundrum. Return the paintings, hoping they were originals, and I was doing the art world a favor but possibly placing myself in jeopardy. Or keep them hidden.

~ ~ ~

As my grief slowly lifted, I realized it had been weeks since I mailed the art stolen from the Elizabeth Kent Oakes Museum in Boston to a couple living in Cincinnati, and as yet, I'd seen no announcement that the lost paintings had been returned to the museum.

When I'd asked Agatha who the Neumans were, her response had been unsatisfactory, to say the least. "Think of them as intermediaries. That's all you need to know."

But they weren't very good intermediaries if they didn't return the paintings.

I'd not yet made any returns myself, putting that off day to day as I debated the wisdom of doing anything. After all, the paintings were safe, and since no one knew I had them, there was no rush. Besides, I needed time to adjust to being completely on my own. To not having Agatha and Stanley to back me up, to visit on the weekends, to talk to on the phone, to spend the approaching holidays with, to love, to share . . .

I stopped the thought in its tracks. Better to focus on my current life. Which was going quite well, if I didn't let myself dwell on my losses, and I ignored my own failure to return the paintings left in my care. Instead, I focused more and more on the fact the Neumans had failed to return the paintings Agatha had entrusted to them. The more I thought about it, the more upset I became.

After a sleepless night, I got up and, despite gritty eyes, spent time on the computer searching out whatever I could about the Neumans. I couldn't be sure which Norman Neuman was the right one, but the most likely candidate had to be the Norman Neuman who recovered lost art and antiquities.

I checked for an address and discovered one that matched where I'd mailed the paintings, an area of Cincinnati called Indian Hill. The Google street view showed an imposing house surrounded by equally imposing grounds, much like Agatha and Stanley's house.

I sat back, feeling exhausted, trying to think how to approach the problem. Drive to Cincinnati, check out the address, maybe chat with a neighbor or two? Although, I doubted that neighborhood would give me many opportunities for that sort of interaction. But I needed to do something.

I dragged through the rest of the day, but I slept soundly that night and awoke with the decision made. For better or worse, I was going to Cincinnati. I'd figure out what to do once I was there.

~ ~ ~

The address I had for the Neumans was on the east side of Cincinnati. With the help of GPS, it took three hours to drive there from my condo. The Neuman house was located in rolling country, surrounded by homes set well back from the street, all of them neatly and expensively cared for. As I'd anticipated, just like our house in Indianapolis, there was no way I could park the car, stroll down the street, and casually bump into either Norman or his neighbors.

I passed the house, drove a short distance, then turned around. On this pass, I noticed the FOR SALE sign in the front yard. That made it easier. I parked and called the real estate agent listed on the sign. Within thirty minutes, she pulled up behind me, and five minutes after that, I was inside the house.

Since I'd told the agent I was an art restorer, she was full of information about the owner and his exploits recovering lost and stolen art. I paid special attention to the paintings on the walls, but quickly realized they weren't going to tell me anything. Although the pictures were above the starving-artist grade, they weren't far enough above to merit my consideration.

The house seemed lightly furnished, but the agent soon covered that with her constant commentary.

"Mr. Neuman recently remarried, and he and his new wife, her name is Josephine, have moved to Brookside Retirement Community. Such a smart thing for them to do. I don't believe the new wife wanted to live here. She's quite an art collector, you know. So compatible, the two of them. He finds lost art, and she's an art lover. It was a real stroke of luck they met."

By the time the real estate agent had given up Josephine's name and mentioned the Neumans' move to Brookside, I'd made it through only the downstairs of the house. Agatha always told me I was much too abrupt, but I saw little point to stringing people along. I'd already taken more advantage of the agent than was fair.

Now that I carry a phone, I always have a built-in way of ending interactions in a manner that even Agatha approved of. I pulled the phone out, pretending it had vibrated, and glanced at the screen. "Oh, I have another appointment."

"But you haven't seen the upstairs. The master bedroom suite is quite impressive. And the grounds—"

"Sorry. Perhaps I can come back later?"

"Yes, of course. Let me give you my card. Just call me. Anytime. Keep in mind, though, this is a very desirable property. If you have any interest, you should move quickly."

"I will." It wasn't precisely a lie. Had I any interest, I would have moved quickly. "Thank you." Waving my phone at her, I hurried back to my car.

After making a sufficient number of turns to avoid any further interaction with the real estate agent, I pulled into an office building parking lot and did a search for the address of Brookside Retirement Community. Fifteen minutes later, I drove past a gatehouse that overlooked rather than guarded the entrance to the Brookside community. I parked near what I took to be the main building, climbed out of the car, and looked around. Easy to tell, this was a place for those who'd planned their retirements with care.

The main building was three stories. The rest of the extensive campus was dotted with individual houses, some finished, some under construction, and some of them quite large. Apparently, not all retirements required downsizing.

Since I didn't know precisely where the Neumans lived, I entered the main building to ask. A real live gatekeeper a.k.a. receptionist was stationed at a desk near the door. As I approached her, a large woman dressed in a bright green-and-yellow outfit that floated around her as if she'd just done a pirouette walked up to me and smiled, as if in recognition.

"Why, hello there." Her voice was fruity and resonant.

I glanced behind me, thinking she had to be addressing someone else. Since there was no one there, it meant she was talking to me. I tried not to roll my eyes, which is a bad habit, according to Agatha. Instead, I nodded at the woman and turned toward the receptionist.

"Can I help you?" the receptionist said.

"Ah . . . I'm here to visit Norman Neuman. Could you tell me which unit he's in?"

"Oh, I can help you with that," trilled the large woman. I thought she'd walked on by, but now discovered she'd paused to eavesdrop.

She walked over and grabbed my hand, pulling me away from the receptionist, who shrugged. "Myrtle Grabinowitz at your service, my dear. Are you Norman's granddaughter, perchance?"

"No."

"Ah, a friend then?"

"Um . . . yes. A friend."

She gestured toward a second person who was now approaching the front door. A black woman, as thin as a stick.

"Yoo-hoo, Lillian. Come meet . . ." The large woman turned back to me. "What did you say your name was, dear?"

"I didn't."

Lillian appeared to be more intelligent than this Myrtle person. I appealed to her with a look Agatha had taught me, and she responded by cocking her head.

"Oh. I thought you did," Myrtle said. "Well, what is it?"

I tried to pull my hand free, but found she was holding me firmly. "Um . . . it's Madeline Scott."

"How lovely of you to visit. Lillian and I would be more than happy to accompany you to the Neumans'. Wouldn't we, Lillian?" Before the other woman could respond, Myrtle focused back on me. "You have a car?"

"Well . . . yes."

"Good. We always welcome a chance to visit Josephine, and since she's moved into one of the cottages, it's become much more difficult. We can't walk that far, you see. But come along. It'll take only a minute to drive there."

I'd begun to regret my hasty action in coming to Brookside without a plan. I believe the saying is "curiosity killed the cat." And that was what brought me to this point. Curiosity. And being taken in tow by this Myrtle Grabino-something-or-other and her sidekick on the way to satisfying that curiosity was an iffy plan, to say the least.

The Neumans could be dangerous. After all, they'd been sent paintings worth hundreds of millions of dollars. They might very well want to hide that fact from the rest of the world. And if they discovered I was the only one who knew about the paintings, they might decide getting rid of me was an excellent plan.

Beginning to panic, I remembered my phone. With a firm jerk, I retrieved my hand from Myrtle's, pulled out my phone, and pretended to look at it. "Sorry. There's been an emergency at work. I need to get there right away."

"Humph. Never get a free minute, you young people with your phones. Always something happening you have to attend to. Where do you work?"

"Oh, I'm an . . . assistant, and the woman I work for is very demanding."

"Well, you can come back anytime. Just ask for me, Myrtle Grabinowitz, and I can take you to Josephine and Norman's."

I considered, very briefly, offering to drop her off at the Neumans' as a way of finding out exactly where they lived. But then I realized she would immediately mention me to them, which would eliminate any possibility of surprising them into confessing. I just wished I'd given a fake name. Hopefully she'd already forgotten.

"Thanks for your help." I ran the words together, and then spun around and jogged out the door.

I know. I know. I should have come up with a plan before I arrived in Cincinnati. And absent that, I should have figured out something before walking into Brookside and announcing my intention to visit the Neumans.

Thoroughly annoyed with myself, I drove toward the highway, where I found an acceptable motel. I spent the evening attempting to formulate a plan, without making much progress.

~ ~ ~

The next morning, I awoke with an idea. It wasn't yet organized enough to be called a plan, but it was better than the lurching from place to place I'd done the day before.

I ate a leisurely breakfast at Bob Evans, then entered the address for the Cincinnati Art Museum into my GPS. It was located in an area called Mount Adams, which I discovered was, in actual fact, a large hill overlooking the Ohio River and downtown Cincinnati.

The museum wouldn't be open for another hour, so I parked and wandered around the area, stopping near a reflecting pool down the hill from the museum. Abundant leaves softened the path around the pond. I shuffled through them, enjoying the crisp sound, and discovered an additional overlook of the river and northern Kentucky. I took a seat on one of the park benches and watched runners and bicyclists whiz past with that view as the backdrop.

At eleven, I returned to the museum. General admission was free, so I spent an hour wandering the galleries before returning to the front desk and asking if it would be possible to meet the museum director. When I introduced myself as an art restorer visiting Cincinnati, I was granted an immediate appointment.

Miriam O'Pinsky was younger than I was expecting. With a wide smile, she walked around her desk to greet me. "We haven't met, but I know you by reputation," she said, extending a hand.

I felt a brief flash of alarm. "You do?"

"We recently had an exhibit where we had an art restorer working in one of our galleries so the public could see what was involved. Your name was suggested by one of the staff, and I did some checking before one of our current restorers agreed to take on the task."

We smiled at each other while I searched for what to say next. I don't interact with people much. Perhaps that's what makes my profession so satisfying. Or perhaps I picked my profession because it meant I didn't have to interact much.

"I'd love to give you a behind-the-scenes tour," Miriam said, obviously much more at ease than I was. "But unfortunately I have a board meeting in a few minutes. However, if you'd like a tour, I could ask one of our curators to show you around."

"Oh. Yes. I'd like that."

What I wanted to do was ask Miriam what she knew about Norman Neuman. Or even if she knew him. But such a question would be impossible to just blurt out, so I opted for sticking around and meeting more of the staff as an alternate strategy. If that didn't work, I might have to work out a dialogue and ask for a second meeting with Miriam.

"Let me give Devi McElroy a call," Miriam said, returning to her desk.

We chatted briefly about art restoration while we waited for Devi, who arrived promptly. She was an attractive young woman approximately my age, and she had that shiny black hair so many Asian women do. After I awkwardly said goodbye to Miriam, Devi directed me to a set of stairs leading to the basement area of the museum. She first used her keycard and then pressed her thumb to a reader in order to access the vaults. That security consciousness gave me a starting point.

"You have good security." I offered the obvious statement, hoping it didn't make me sound like an idiot.

"Every museum takes more care these days. Surely you're familiar with the Elizabeth Kent Oakes robbery?"

I could have hugged her for bringing that up. It meant I didn't have to spend all my time with her dancing around the subject.

"Of course," I said. "Everyone even marginally associated with the art world knows about that. I wonder if it'll ever be solved."

She gave me a thoughtful glance. "It could be. One just never knows."

I spoke quickly before I lost my nerve. "I've heard Norman Neuman's been trying to solve the case for years."

She turned a full-on smile at me. "You know Norman?"

*Wow.* I hadn't expected to hit pay dirt so quickly. But since I had, I needed to pay attention and think quickly. "Only by reputation. I've admired him from afar."

"Did you know he lives in this area?"

I debated . . . would I be expected to know that, or not? I decided on *not*. "Really? That's so cool. I'd love to meet him." What I'd do or say if that happened, I had no idea. But that was why I came to Cincinnati, after all.

"Norman is married to a very good friend of mine. If I call her, I know Josephine would be happy to have us over for tea," Devi said, continuing to grin.

"That would be . . . wonderful. If it's not too much trouble."

"Josephine and Norman are dedicated to art, and since you help restore masterpieces, I know they'd love to meet you. In fact, let me give her a call right now, although we'll have to go back upstairs. No signal down here."

I followed in Devi's wake and stood to one side while she spoke with Josephine. When the conversation ended with "We'll see you then," I knew an invitation had been extended.

Devi turned to me, smiling. "She said for us to come over about four. I hope that works for you?"

"It does."

"Great. Well, let's get back to that tour, shall we?"

From that point on, I had difficulty concentrating on what she was showing me. I had to keep pinching my wrist to force myself to focus.

~ ~ ~

It was rare for me to think of doing something like inviting Devi to lunch when my personal tour ended at one thirty. So I was proud of myself, but relieved, when she begged off. We parted, agreeing to meet at Josephine and Norman's house at four. She gave me the address, along with specific directions to their house, so there would be no more encounters with large, fluttery women who wouldn't let go of my hand.

If the Neumans were planning to keep the art, they sure wouldn't be willing to tell me about it. Maybe all I could expect would be to get a read on their characters, although I'm not particularly adept at that. Agatha tried to help me, but I have a tendency to be literal, and often that leads to misunderstandings.

Following Devi's instructions, I parked near the Neumans' driveway right before four o'clock and sat waiting for her to arrive. She did so within five minutes, and together we walked to the front door.

The woman who answered the door wasn't young, but was still slender and healthy looking. Her hair, which she wore in a smooth bob, was a mix of dark brown and gray that suited her slightly severe expression. That expression changed abruptly when she turned to greet Devi with the same expression Agatha used to get whenever I visited. It meant Devi and Josephine were, indeed, very good friends.

Josephine turned to me and offered a hand, along with what I've learned is a social smile. That was okay, though. I didn't expect her to be all that thrilled to meet me.

"Madeline Scott?" She frowned, but I was pretty sure it meant she was thinking, not that she was angry. "Are you by any chance related to Agatha and Stanley Scott?"

*Uh-oh.* I should have realized the Neumans would immediately connect me to Agatha and Stanley. "I'm their daughter."

I knew the pause before I answered had been overly long, but I hoped it hadn't been too long. And I hoped I'd sounded believable, because saying I was Agatha and Stanley's daughter was not precisely true, at least not in the biological sense.

I could see Josephine was doing the math, trying to match my relative youth to Agatha's age. "Adopted," I said, not wanting to go into the details. Details, at any rate, that were mostly a mystery.

Josephine's perplexed expression cleared. "Of course. Please come in. Norman isn't here at the moment, but he'll be back soon."

"Why don't I make tea while you two get acquainted," Devi said.

"Thank you, dear."

I thought Devi and Josephine were acting more like close relatives than simply friends. And I do know there is nothing simple about friendship.

Josephine ushered me into a living room furnished with Scandinavian furniture. Very good paintings hung on two of the walls, but a third wall was noticeably bare. None of the paintings I'd mailed them were in evidence, although I suppose that was asking far too much. If they were going to keep the art, surely they'd hang it out of sight. The way Agatha and Stanley had.

Suddenly, I was overwhelmed by the knowledge that Stanley had been a thief. And a forger. Tears stung my eyes, so I focused on one of the paintings until I could be sure I'd squelched the impulse to cry. Josephine gestured for me to sit on the sofa and silently took a seat facing me. It wasn't until I lifted my gaze that she spoke.

"I didn't know Agatha and Stanley had any children. And you're an art restorer, Devi said?"

"Yes." I fiddled with my hands, trying to figure out what else to say. Agatha had often gone through simple dialogues to help me through awkward pauses like this one. I tried to remember one now.

"You have a lovely home." There. Agatha had always insisted that was a crowd-pleaser as everyone loves to have their home praised, even when it was a mess.

But the compliment was truer of the Neumans' home than for those of my few acquaintances. A colorful Oriental rug delineated the area where we were seated from the hardwood floor. The couch was a silvery gray, and the chair where Josephine was seated was a soft shade of maroon. The end tables and coffee table were teak, and everything had a clean, unfussy appearance.

At that moment, Devi reappeared carrying a tray with a pot of tea, cups, and a plate of cookies, which she deposited on the coffee table. She knelt down to pour the tea.

"I chose that Osmanthus Chin Hsuan tea," she said with a smile toward Josephine. "Mainly because I love the tin it comes in. It's a pinkish bronze with a cherry tree motif," she added, handing me my cup.

"What brings you to Cincinnati?" Josephine asked as I lifted my cup to take a sip.

I swallowed, trying to come up with an answer other than *I'm here to find out what you and your husband have done with the Elizabeth Kent Oakes art.*

I was saved from answering by the sound of a door opening, followed by the appearance of a man in the doorway. Josephine stood and greeted him with a kiss, and she had that same expression on her face she'd had when greeting Devi. So this must be Norman. He was also trim and fit with mostly silver hair and intelligent eyes.

I tried to decide if he looked like the kind of man who would accept stolen art and then kill anyone who might expose him. Stanley always talked about having gut feelings about people, but I had no idea what he meant by that. It sounded like an uncomfortable proposition. To my eyes, this man didn't appear any more unscrupulous or shifty than Agatha and Stanley. Of course, I was blinded by my love for Agatha and Stanley. Perhaps they seemed shifty to other people.

By the time Norman had been introduced and Devi had fetched a cup for him, I'd had time to prepare an answer to Josephine's question about what brought me to Cincinnati.

"I'm here to assess a painting to see if it can be restored," I said, trying not to squirm. I really don't like making things up, although Agatha tried to teach me the whys and hows of doing it in social situations.

"Can you share the client's name?" Norman asked.

My mind was a total blank, so I was forced to go with the truth. "No, I'm afraid I can't."

"Have you seen the painting yet?" Devi asked.

"No. Not yet." Again, the truth worked.

We all took sips of tea, and an uncomfortable silence settled over us until Josephine, with a quick glance at Norman, set her cup down with a definitive click. "And how are your parents?"

"Oh. They . . . passed away." I found myself struggling to swallow around a huge lump in my throat and blinked rapidly, trying to fend off tears.

"I'm sorry to hear that," Josephine said.

She sounded brisk, which was fine. I never know what to say when someone gives me one of those funny looks full of squinty eyes and tightened lips, and says they're sorry my parents died. Not that there were many people in my life to do that. A couple of Agatha's nurses and the attorney was all.

"Recently?" Josephine asked.

"Yes."

"In Indianapolis?"

"No. I mean, yes. Stanley died in Indianapolis."

I hesitated, finding myself unsure of how much to tell them. There might be a greater reason for Agatha to insist we go to Colorado when she was dying besides wanting to see the mountains. But I couldn't imagine what it might be.

I cleared my throat. "Agatha, she, uh, died in Colorado."

Josephine sat back, her eyebrows lifting, then lowering.

"Did you know them?" Suddenly, it was important to me to know if they were merely acquaintances or if I was in the company of someone who knew Agatha and Stanley well.

"I only met them the one time," Josephine replied. "I liked them. At least, I liked Agatha. I spoke only briefly with Stanley."

I don't know why such a simple statement would be my undoing. Devi moved quickly, taking my arm and directing me to a bathroom.

It was a while before I was able to face them again. My eyes were still red, and I was dreadfully uncomfortable, but at least I no longer felt like crying. I forced myself to re-enter the room.

"I need to be going," I told them.

"You can't." Devi jumped up and came over, took me by the hand, and led me back to a seat on the couch. "You see, we have an important question for you." She turned to Norman, who nodded. "We want to know what you know about the paintings your parents mailed to Josephine and Norman."

The question left me disoriented and feeling slightly dizzy. It was so exactly the question I wanted to ask them. Or mostly it was. The four of us sat staring at one another while I searched for something to say.

I was starting to tremble, as if I were outside in the cold without a coat. "H-how did you know the paintings came from my parents?"

Since I'd been the one to mail them, I knew the return address was a fake. As well, the person whose name appeared with that fake address was also a fake. Agatha had suggested the name. Leonardo D. Vincent. *Really?*

"We saw the paintings when we visited your parents last August," Josephine said. "And they discussed having us help return them."

I supposed that was when Agatha had been auditioning them as possible recipients of the paintings, and they must have passed whatever tests she'd devised. Unfortunately, she'd run out of time to arrange the return of the rest of the paintings. She'd left that up to me to figure out.

While I was thinking all that, the three of them watched me. It was unnerving.

At some point, I'd picked up my cup of tea. I now set it down. I was annoyed at being made to feel like I was the one in the wrong here. I sort of was, I suppose. Although I'd been perfectly innocent until I truly grasped what Agatha and Stanley had been up to. "Why haven't you returned the paintings to the museum?"

"We have returned them," Josephine said.

"Then why no announcement?" I knew the return would be a major news story, or it should be.

"The museum wanted to authenticate the paintings before telling anyone they'd been returned," Norman said.

"And there's been a glitch," Josephine added. "The most valuable painting turned out to be a fake, and the FBI suspects us of arranging the forgery."

My heart rate shot up, and my mouth dried out. I took a quick sip of tea, but since I was still shaking, I hastily returned the cup, with a slight rattle, to its saucer.

Devi turned to me. "Do you know where the original might be?"

"Which painting is it?" I was stalling for time, wishing I could stop the shaking and slow the pounding of my heart. I was pretty sure I knew which one they were talking about. The only one of the eight I'd seen Stanley copy. It had been so long ago, my art education had barely begun, and I'd forgotten it until this moment.

"*Storm on the Sea of Galilee*," Norman said.

A headache added itself to the rest of my physical discomforts. I looked down at my teacup, so I wouldn't have to face them.

"Sorry. I have no idea where it might be." Actually, I had an idea, but I doubted there was any way I could find out for sure without taking a risk.

"What about the other paintings?" Norman said. "I noticed several other stolen paintings in your parents' collection, besides the Elizabeth Kent Oakes ones. Do you know what happened to them?"

"I don't." I'm a terrible liar, so as I spoke, I continued to look down. "They may still be at the house, I suppose."

"Do you have a key?"

I shook my head, remembering Agatha telling me not to return to the house because it might be unsafe. Given what I now knew, that may have been an understatement. But it had been no hardship. Despite living there nearly twenty years, I felt little connection to the house, which I'd always thought of as vaguely threatening. I was glad not to have any responsibility for it. And not to have to worry about any remaining evidence it possibly contained of Stanley's illegal activities.

"You had to know, though, that your parents had stolen art on their walls. After all, you're an art restorer," Josephine said.

I shook my head, struggling to find something true to say about Stanley. "Stanley . . . he liked to copy masterpieces. He always said it was the poor man's version of the Louvre." Except, he hadn't been poor, and I now doubted that all the pictures on our walls had been copies.

"So you're saying all the paintings we saw were forgeries?" Norman said. "But that can't be true, given the rest of the art was authenticated. Unless . . ."

"What, love?" Josephine said.

"Unless all of them are fakes and the authenticators missed it."

"Is that even possible?" Devi said. "Given the one painting was exposed as a fake, wouldn't they recheck their work?"

Norman nodded. "I expect that's exactly what they're doing. It's probably the reason we haven't heard from Rosenberg and Collins for a while."

"And why the museum hasn't yet announced their return," Josephine said.

Listening to them, I knew exactly what I had to do. I needed to get back to Indianapolis and take a much closer look at the paintings entrusted to me. And I needed to get into the house and see if there were any more paintings.

As a child, I'd discovered several hiding places. I'd always shared my finds with Stanley, who'd acted delighted with my cleverness. Now, looking back on that with adult eyes, I doubt he'd been delighted. I also wondered if Agatha had known about the hiding places.

"Madeline could talk to them," Devi said.

I'd lost track of the conversation and wasn't sure who the "them" were.

"Agents Rosenberg and Collins." Devi stared at me intently. "You could tell them about Agatha and Stanley. Corroborate that Norman and Josephine got the paintings from them. Let the FBI figure out the rest."

Oh no, I couldn't do that. I shook my head, my heart pounding.

I couldn't get anywhere near an FBI agent. Not while I was in possession of stolen paintings. Or possible stolen paintings. And I'd better figure out which they were, and fast. And who knew what might still be hidden in the house? If the FBI learned about me, wouldn't they immediately get a search warrant?

No. I had to get back to Indianapolis. Right now.

I pulled out my phone. "Sorry. I need to go. There's an emergency." I grabbed my purse off the floor and hurried out the door. I must have taken them all by surprise, because nobody moved to stop me.

## Chapter Twenty-Two

### Myrtle

The Mekyles hesitated in the doorway, and I waved them over. Ever since Bertie decided he liked Delores better than me, I've had to work a bit harder to snag dinner companions. It's most aggravating, but darned if I'm going to sit by myself, like Edna often does.

Of course, that makes her my court of last resort. If I can't catch the attention of someone I like, I can always join her. She doesn't seem to mind either way. I must say, I rather envy her that independence.

But tonight, I'm all set since Malcolm and Thelma have made their way to my table and sat down. I also took pity on Edna and invited her to join us.

"I'm so glad you're all here, since I have a delicious piece of news for you." I wasn't entirely certain who the young lady was who'd asked for Norman, but I can speculate with the best of them, if I do say so. And although my news was over twenty-four hours old—the delay caused by one of my granddaughters taking me to dinner last night—I still think it's worth sharing.

"Norman had a most interesting visitor yesterday," I told them.

"Another FBI agent?" Thelma said. It was an excellent guess, although an easy one, since I'd shared all about my interrogation with them.

"She was possibly too young. Of course, I expect there are young FBI agents. Not all of them can be middle-aged, can they?"

"I believe they recruit college graduates," Malcolm said, waving away the waitress's attempt to serve him a salad.

"You really need more greens in your diet," Thelma said.

"I'm not a horse, am I?" He sounded quite sharp, which surprised me. He and Thelma had always seemed . . . well, not affectionate, but at least willing to peacefully put up with each other.

Edna and I exchanged a look.

Thelma sniffed and sat back so the girl could place a salad in front of her. I confess, salad is not my favorite part of the meal. Dessert is. But I do know I should eat *some* vegetables.

"So, this girl. What did she look like?" Malcolm asked after the waitress moved on.

"Short brown hair, all bouncy curls. Very nice skin. She must have excellent genes. A pretty little thing, although she's a bit plumper than she should be. And those glasses need to go." Actually, the mysterious girl was very pretty. And yes, I do know my beauty-contest days are behind me, but I declare, I do still cut an attractive figure. My hair is always perfectly styled and my lipstick fresh. Unlike some people.

"Did you catch her name?" Edna asked.

"I most certainly did. Madeline Scott."

Malcolm's water glass wobbled. He set it back down and grabbed a napkin to mop up the splash on his bread plate. Then he and Thelma exchanged a glance that intrigued me.

"You know her?" I watched the two of them carefully.

"Nope. Never heard of her." Malcolm picked up his glass of water again with a hand that trembled slightly.

I tried to remember if I'd noticed him having a tremor before. I didn't believe I had.

Thelma bent her head over her salad. They were both acting oddly, but for the life of me, I couldn't figure out why.

Unless . . .

"You could be right, you know," I said, puzzling it out. "She could have something to do with the FBI."

Again, Malcolm and Thelma exchanged a look.

"Surely not," Edna said, at the same moment that Thelma said, "I doubt that,"

Then Thelma changed the subject, and when I tried to circle back, she said she had a terrible headache and perhaps, if I didn't mind, she and Malcolm would skip dessert. Well, I certainly wasn't going to skip dessert. It was cheesecake. I never skip cheesecake.

"That was extremely odd," I told Edna once the Mekyles left the table.

"I agree," Edna said. "Maybe we should tell Josephine." She pushed away her plate with half the cheesecake still on it.

"Aren't you going to eat that?" I do hate seeing something so delicious go to waste.

"I mean it," Edna said as she moved her cheesecake in my direction, "about telling Josephine. She does seem to attract odd goings-on."

"She does, at that. But I doubt there's a need to bother her with something so insignificant."

"Of course. You're right," Edna said.

But she had a calculating look on her face, and I was pretty sure she was as intrigued by Madeline Scott's visit as I was.

# Chapter Twenty-Three

## *Josephine*

I answered the door to find Myrtle on my doorstep. It seems like I've seen more of her since moving out of the main building than when she lived down the hall. And it's odd, because I'll bet Myrtle has never given one thought to joining the ten-thousand-steps-a-day club. I peered around her to see the shuttle bus turning the corner. Obviously, Myrtle had hijacked it for her personal excursion.

"Josephine, I just had to talk to you. Is Norman here?"

We'd both been eating breakfast. Reluctantly, I ushered her in. But then, what other choice did I have with her transportation beating a hasty retreat?

"A cup of tea?" I said.

"Absolutely. I love your tea. And I wouldn't say no to a cookie."

Of course she wouldn't. The woman has been cultivating an extremely intimate relationship with cookies for quite some time.

I poured her a cup of tea and placed four cookies on a small plate in front of her.

"So, what is it you need to tell us?"

"It's about that young woman who came to visit Norman the other day."

I frowned at her. How on earth did she know about that? Then I remembered Lill's report that Myrtle had been present when Madeline first arrived at Brookside.

"I tried to tell her I'd show her where you live, but her phone rang. She said she'd come back later. So, did she?"

"Did she tell you her name?"

"Madeline Scott. I remember because I have a granddaughter named Madeline, and she married Steve Scott. But this woman wasn't my granddaughter, of course." Myrtle lifted her chin, then nodded. I think if she could have managed it, she would have patted herself on the back.

"She said she wasn't your granddaughter, Norman, so I didn't really think much more about it. But when I shared the news about her visit with the Mekyles at dinner, they reacted so oddly."

"In what way?" I asked.

"I think they recognized her name, and not because they have a granddaughter with that name. And then Thelma said she had a headache, and they left before dessert was served. And it was cheesecake."

"I agree, that is strange." I had my tongue in my cheek, but Myrtle didn't notice. Norman did and twinkled at me.

"I believe it's all part of the stolen art mystery."

"Stolen art mystery?" I said.

"Yes. First, you receive mysterious packages. Then the FBI interviews me about those packages. And now this stranger has shown up. It all ties together. We have to call Agent Rosenkrantz and alert him."

*Really?* She could remember Madeline's name with perfect clarity but mangle the FBI agent's name?

"That isn't necessary," I said, my thoughts scrambling. "We met with Madeline later."

"Yes," Norman said. "She's . . . the daughter of friends. She's visiting Cincinnati, and I promised her parents I'd show her around."

"Oh." Myrtle seemed to deflate. "Are you sure?"

"Of course I'm sure," Norman said.

During this exchange, Myrtle had munched her way through the cookies I'd put out, and was now peering around as if expecting more to jump on the plate.

I spoke quickly. "I need to leave for a doctor's appointment, so I can drive you back."

Norman shot me a glance filled with gratitude, and I knew I'd be collecting my reward later.

I went to get my purse and keys. I didn't know how she was doing it, but Myrtle seemed to be tuned in on a cosmic level to everything going on with us and the Elizabeth Kent Oakes art. It was unnerving, given I was so used to her clueless vagueness.

And until Norman and I were no longer persons of interest to the FBI, Myrtle's poking around the edges of our personal mystery was unwelcome, to say the least.

And why did the Mekyles keep appearing at unexpected intervals in the same narrative?

~ ~ ~

I dropped Myrtle off, then drove home. Norman was at work on the computer. He barely looked up to greet me, which was unusual.

I didn't care, however, because I was on a mission of my own. I sat down at the other computer and typed the name of the play Malcolm had said was his favorite. Although the phrase brought up possibilities, none of them was a play. I then searched on the purported playwright's name. Still nothing.

I tried searching on Broadway plays, and found a site, *Broadway World*, which listed plays by the year. Still nothing.

Then I typed in "Malcolm Mekyle." Nowhere in Google's massive database did a Malcolm Mekyle reside. I went to check on Norman and found him staring at his computer screen.

"You didn't find any Mekyles?" I said, already knowing the answer.

"I did not."

"I tried to find the play Malcolm mentioned."

"And you discovered?"

"It doesn't seem to exist either. Is that what's known as a clue?"

Norman's intent expression indicated that, like me, he was doing a complex calculation.

"So," I said. "Do you think Malcolm Mekyle is the Malcolm that Agatha mentioned when we arrived in Indianapolis?" I'd finally remembered where I'd heard the name before. "Except he had a different last name, didn't he? Jones . . . or Johnson maybe?"

"Johannsen," Norman said.

"Do you know him?"

"Only by reputation. We've never met."

"Or maybe you have. If Malcolm Johanssen and Malcolm Mekyle are the same person, it's possible he and Thelma are on the trail of the Elizabeth Kent Oakes art. But how did they find out about us?"

"From Agatha, I expect."

"Why would Agatha have told them?" I sifted through facts and conjectures.

"Remember, she mentioned Malcolm's name to us, as an aside. Likely she did the same to him, when she let him know we'd aced him out."

"But how did they get into Brookside so quickly if the first they heard about us was when they heard about us from Agatha?"

"With Brookside's expansion, there's no longer a waiting list. They were probably able to walk right in the door."

"But what good is it? Them following us around."

"Obviously not much," Norman said. "But with that large a reward at stake, I expect they're grasping at any straw. And if he was the Malcolm summoned by Agatha and Stanley, and like you, I believe he is, he might know enough to also consider Madeline a lead."

It was hardly reassuring news. "She lives in Indianapolis?" I said.

"She does."

"Guess I know what we're doing today."

Norman stood and finally remembered he owed me for removing Myrtle. "That's one of the things I love about you, Jo.

You're more than a match for the Myrtles and Mekyles of the world."

Which earned him a punch—a soft one—on the arm.

# Chapter Twenty-Four

## *Maddie*

On the drive home, I had time to think about how I was going to get into the house. The executor had mentioned he'd changed the locks the last time we met, but I figured I could talk him into lending me a key, if he had one. Unless Agatha had specifically instructed him not to.

If he wouldn't give me the key, I'd just have to break in.

When I stopped for gas, I called the executor's office and made an appointment to meet with him first thing the next morning.

~ ~ ~

I thought about my strategy as I left the executor's office, the key clutched in my hand. He'd required very little convincing to turn it over. A few carefully rehearsed words about needing time to bid both Agatha and Stanley farewell, as well as a comment that I'd left some of my artwork behind, did the trick.

I decided I didn't need to creep into the house in the dark of night. Better to act as if I still lived there. And if I did run into somebody, I could trot out the same excuses for my visit that had worked on the executor. For all I knew, nobody even realized that Stanley and Agatha were dead, as I'd not arranged for obituaries to appear in the newspaper.

What I hadn't counted on was the driveway gate being closed and locked. The only key I had was to the front door. It meant I had to park on the street and walk in. Not my preferred approach. Still, the gate only served to block the driveway. I simply walked around one of the two brick pillars, through a gap in the hedge, then up to the front door.

The house was nearly as cold inside as the wintry air was outside, and it smelled musty, which wasn't surprising as it had been vacant since Agatha and I had left for Colorado. Since I'd usually entered from the back door, it felt strange coming in this way. For a moment, I stood, taking in the high ceiling with its wood paneling. An ornate chandelier hung from a twenty-foot chain, but was still ten feet above my head. I switched it on, and most of the dark shadows silently receded. Shivering, I took a deep breath, then began my search.

The first hiding place I checked was in the conservatory. The room, with its many windows, was bright enough to see that the plants in smaller pots were dead, and those in the larger containers were dying. The furniture remained but was pushed to one side, I suspect when the Oriental rug was removed. The hidden space in here yielded nothing but dust and the desiccated carcass of a mouse.

The second spot, behind the staircase, near the elevator, contained a figurine and a cardboard tube. I pulled both items out and left them at the bottom of the staircase before going upstairs to the room that had been my bedroom. The hiding place here was to the left of the fireplace, and it was large enough for a person of modest proportions to fit inside. I knew this since I'd hidden there once during a game of hide-and-seek.

I used my phone to illuminate the interior, revealing half a dozen cardboard tubes propped in the corner. Thankful there was little dust, I was reaching for the first one when I heard a steady pounding and realized someone was knocking on the front door.

I hurried across the hall to the room that overlooked the front door. A man and a woman stood on the porch with their backs to me. The woman was tall, the man short. She turned to speak to the man, and I could see her face. I didn't recognize her.

I waited for the two to give up and leave. Instead, they stepped off the porch and split up, circling the house in different directions. The next sound I heard was of breaking glass. I pulled my phone out to dial 9-1-1 before deciding against it.

Instead, I crossed back to my room and waited in the doorway, listening for any further sounds. I knew the staircase had treads that squeaked, which would warn me if the two started upstairs. But before I heard any squeaks, I heard the man's voice. The words were clear, although the tone was soft.

"Well, just lookee here."

"What is it?" The second voice, the woman's, was equally clear, a feature of the acoustics in the main hall.

"Why, I believe this is an Egyptian bronze, and this tube . . . it's most promising."

"Why on earth would they just be lying here by the stairs?"

With a jolt, I realized they were talking about the tube and figurine I'd left at the bottom of the stairs so I could pick them up on my way out.

"Perhaps someone's here?"

"We made enough racket with our knocking. If someone were here, they'd have come to the door."

"Not if their purpose is similar to ours." The man lowered his voice further, and I couldn't make out his next words. But I'd heard enough.

I crept across the room, slipped into the cavity beside the fireplace, and pulled the panel shut. It clicked into place, but the couple were far enough away they couldn't have heard it.

It might not have been dusty, but the space quickly became stuffy. I pulled my phone out and was reassured that it would provide light, if I needed it. Although I rarely get calls, I made sure the ringer was turned off. I wouldn't put it past the two people currently roaming the house searching for treasure to rip into a wall if they heard an unusual sound.

That thought brought me a moment of unease, but I decided to trust in whoever had built this secret niche, given how well they'd camouflaged both it and the part of the carving that opened it.

Voices approached. I couldn't make out the words at first, but then I could.

"Do you think there could be a secret room somewhere?" the woman said. "All this carving. You remember that time in Italy, don't you?"

"I do. You had to tap or twist . . . was it the vase of ivy or something else?"

As footsteps drew closer, I held my breath. Even though I knew they couldn't possibly hear the frantic hammering of my heart, it was difficult not to believe they might.

I needed, badly, to shift my position, but I didn't dare. I forced myself to breathe slowly and deeply, and after a few breaths, my heart slowed.

Meanwhile, I could hear one, or both, of them tapping on the paneling. I clicked on my phone to search for a way to jam or hold the panel in place should they stumble across the right spot. At that thought, my heart rate spiked again. There was a sudden knock in the vicinity of my ear, which made me jump and bang the phone against the wall.

"Listen," the man said.

I was practically panting in my effort to get enough oxygen.

"To what?" the woman said.

"I think it's the doorbell?"

"It could be a neighbor. Maybe they saw us."

"Yes, perhaps I'd better answer it," the woman said.

I heard a set of footsteps leaving the room.

The man, I assumed it was the man, gave the panel a couple more halfhearted taps before I heard him leave as well. At least, my exhausted heart hoped they'd both left.

I shifted into a more comfortable position and waited another five minutes before I eased the panel open a crack.

# Chapter Twenty-Five

## *Josephine*

On the way to Indianapolis, Norman talked to the investigator about Madeline while I drove and listened to his half of the conversation.

"So he still can't find any heirs?" I said when Norman ended the call.

"He's going to do some more checking, but he's already discovered there were no probated wills. It means everything was probably left to a trust. And he didn't find any record of the Scotts adopting Madeline. He suggested the possibility she might be a con artist, but I doubt that. She seemed genuinely concerned about the paintings being returned. And how would she even know about them, if she wasn't closely connected to Agatha and Stanley? Plus, I didn't pick up any vibes that she was trying to retrieve the art. Or that she was holding back information."

"I think she was," I told him. "Holding back information, that is."

"What makes you say that?"

I shrugged. "Intuition. I can't point to anything specific."

"Guess we just have to see what we can find out," Norman said.

We drove to Madeline's address, which the investigator had tracked down. It was an upscale condominium complex in a pleasant suburb. She didn't answer her door, and there was no one around we could ask about her. According to Norman, we weren't yet to the point of knocking on her neighbors' doors.

"That leaves us only one option," he said.

I nodded. "Agatha and Stanley's house."

At the Scott house, we found the neighborhood as quiet and seemingly deserted as it had been on our first visit. This time, the gate to the driveway was shut, so we drove around the corner to park. We noticed two other parked cars. One had an Ohio license plate, the other an Indiana plate.

Norman pulled in behind the car with the Indiana plate, and we got out and made our way to the front door. Although the lawn was free of leaves, the house had an abandoned feel to it. Norman rang the doorbell. When there was no response, he knocked. Eventually, we heard steps, and I could see the wavery outline of a tall, thin person approaching the door. When it opened, my mouth also opened, in surprise.

"Thelma, what are you doing here?"

Her eyes had widened upon seeing Norman and me. She flushed and raised a hand to her mouth. "Oh. It's you."

"May we come in?"

"Oh . . . no. I don't believe that's a good idea." She stepped outside and pulled the door almost closed behind her. During that maneuver, I'd felt no warm air escaping from the house.

"Is Malcolm with you, Thelma?" Norman asked.

"Um . . . we're here visiting our niece."

"How nice," I said. "So Madeline's here?"

"Madeline?"

"Isn't that the niece you're talking about? Madeline Scott?"

Thelma frowned. "I'm sorry, I don't know a Madeline Scott. Our niece just bought this house. We're here visiting her. Helping her get settled."

Without turning on the heat? I didn't think so.

"And your niece's name is?" Norman asked with that smile I knew wasn't really a smile.

Thelma's lips thinned, and she shook her head slightly. "It's . . . Bernice."

Norman touched my arm and tipped his head. "Okay then, Thelma. Sorry to have bothered you. Enjoy your visit." He took my arm and propelled me down the steps and away from the house.

I waited until we'd regained the street before speaking. "What's going on?"

"If that woman has a niece named Bernice, I'm a unicorn. It's obvious that when Myrtle mentioned Madeline's visit to them at dinner yesterday, they decided to come," Norman said.

"That means Malcolm is after the art, and he's put two and two together a step further than Myrtle has."

"Nobody but the FBI and us knows that the Rembrandt is still missing, though."

"Remember, Madeline knows," I said. "And I'll bet that's her car, the one with Indiana plates, which means she's probably in that house. Do you think they could be holding her prisoner?"

He shook his head. "I doubt it."

"But why would Thelma answer the door?" I said.

"I expect she figured it was a neighbor checking on who was in the house, and decided it was better to pretend she belonged so the neighbor didn't call the police."

"Too bad for her it was us."

"Indeed."

By that time we were back to our car. We got in and sat watching the house for any further comings and goings.

"Look at that," Norman said. He was watching something in the rearview mirror. I turned to look, just in time to see Thelma and Malcolm getting into the car with Ohio plates and driving off.

"They must have come out the back," Norman said.

"So, where's Madeline?"

"She has to be in the house."

"We ought to check on her." Without waiting for Norman's agreement, I got out and hurried toward the house. Norman caught up, and we checked the front door. Locked. We stepped off the porch and walked around the house. In the back, we found a broken window.

"I'll bet that's how the Mekyles got in. And out," I said. "But why break in? Why not just knock and then push their way in when Madeline answered the door?"

"Maybe she didn't answer the door."

"Which means she could be in the house somewhere. Hiding, maybe?"

"Possibly."

"I'd really like to check on her," I said, eyeing the broken window. "Remember the way the elevator was hidden? Madeline could be inside it, waiting for the Mekyles to leave."

"I'm not breaking in," Norman said. "Let's try knocking again."

Since he has more extensive experience in such matters than I do, although my experience is not insignificant, I walked with him back to the front of the house, and he once more knocked on the front door.

# Chapter Twenty-Six

## *Maddie*

I eased the panel ajar, which let in a stream of cold, fresh air. Breathing it in, I realized I was feeling muzzy in the head. Gradually, the fresh air revived me. I waited another five minutes, listening for the slightest sound, but there was no hint of even the creaking that was normal for the house when the wind picked up.

Finally, I decided it was safe to move. I stepped out into the room, making sure the panel slid back into place behind me. Then I tiptoed over to the doorway and paused once again, listening.

Nothing. The couple must have left.

I peered out my window, which overlooked the back of the house, and then stepped across the hall to check out the front. I was just in time to see a second couple approach the front door from the side of the house. The woman tipped her head, and I recognized her.

Josephine Neuman. That meant the man was probably Norman.

But what were they doing in Indianapolis? And so close on the heels of two people I didn't know. My heart picked up its pace, and while I tried to think what to do, they started knocking.

I waited at the top of the stairs to see if the couple who'd broken in earlier responded. I was tempted to hide again but when nobody appeared, the better plan seemed to be to answer the door and act as if nothing were amiss. I patted my pocket, making sure my phone was where I could quickly access it, then crept down the stairs, noticing, when I reached the bottom, that the figurine and cardboard tube I'd left there were missing. It wasn't something I could do anything about right now, though.

The knocking continued.

When I answered the door, Josephine pushed past Norman and took my hand.

"Thank goodness you're okay."

"Why wouldn't I be okay?" Was she playing some sort of elaborate charade with me? Well, I was not playing.

"When we arrived earlier, we knocked, and we knew the person who answered the door definitely didn't belong here. And after we saw that person and her companion leave, we walked around the house and found a broken window."

"How did you know the person didn't belong?" I asked, addressing only one part of what she was saying that I didn't understand.

"Her name, or at least the name she gave us, is Thelma Mekyle," Josephine said. "Do you know her?"

"No."

"And you haven't sold the house to someone named Bernice?"

"Absolutely not."

"You didn't realize someone else was in the house?" Norman asked.

I was becoming more uncomfortable by the moment. Lying is not one of my skills, even when I'm perfectly calm, but I needed to give it a try. "I was upstairs, looking for something I left behind. This Thelma . . ."

"Mekyle."

"Yes, Mekyle. All I can tell you is that I didn't hear her."

I was beginning to make some calculations, and thought I was rapidly reaching the correct conclusion. This Thelma person and the man with her somehow knew about Stanley and Agatha's art collection, and they were here to grab whatever they could. Of course, I still didn't know how the Neumans knew the Mekyles or how the Mekyles knew Agatha and Stanley, but that part could wait.

Although, it couldn't wait too long since Thelma and her companion had had one bit of success . . . the figurine, along with whatever was concealed in the cardboard tube. And who knew what that might have been? Possibly even the missing Rembrandt. So it was a good thing Josephine and Norman knew who they were.

"You might want to check if anything is missing," Norman said. He settled into a stance that I think meant he had no intention of leaving.

"There's nothing here for them to steal." Which I judged was mostly true, so I was able to say it with appropriate conviction. Before I could stumble into more ill-advised speech, Josephine once again said how relieved she was that I was okay. Then she stepped closer and spoke softly.

"We're on your side, Madeline. And, if it helps, remember that Agatha and Stanley trusted us with some of their secrets, along with the Elizabeth Kent Oakes art."

That part was true. Agatha had sent them the paintings. What I didn't know was whether she trusted them, or whether she'd just run out of time and was grabbing at straws.

Right now, I needed to get rid of them so I could check what was left in the basement gallery.

"We'll be happy to stick around to make sure the Mekyles don't come back," Josephine said, giving me a querying glance.

I don't know why I nodded agreement. But there was something about her that inspired confidence. Perhaps that's what Stanley meant by having a gut reaction.

"And I can see about fixing that broken window," Norman said.

I nodded again. "Thank you."

Norman checked out the window, then looked up directions to a hardware store, gave Josephine a kiss, and said he'd be back in a bit.

"It's chilly in here," Josephine said. "Perhaps I can make us a cup of tea? If I remember right, your mother had quite an imposing tea set."

"Yes. Her Queen Elizabeth teapot is what I called it. But I doubt there's any tea." Or any tea set, for that matter.

"I'll just settle for another look at that gorgeous staircase, then."

"I used to slide down the banister. I can't believe Agatha let me do that."

"What's going to happen with the house? Is it yours now?"

"No, thank goodness. The executor's in charge of it. I'm not sure what his plans are." A slight prevarication, not a total lie. I didn't know for certain what the actual owner, whoever that was, had planned.

By this time, we'd approached the staircase, and Josephine had stepped close to run a finger reverently over the carvings. After a couple of minutes, she glanced up and then walked over to the wall behind which the elevator was located.

"This is particularly amazing. The way the elevator is concealed. It's masterful. It seems to me, one has to touch this flower . . ." She ran a finger over the flower in question, then pushed, and the panel that served as the elevator's door swung open. "Oh my," she said, stepping back. "It's a surprise even when you know it's there, isn't it?"

I should have realized Josephine knew about the elevator, after that comment about being shown Stanley and Agatha's collection. Still, I felt a niggle of unease at the idea of sharing anything more with her.

"Why are you here?" I said, facing her squarely.

"Do you remember the woman you met when you first arrived at Brookside?"

It seemed an odd non-answer to my question, and I had to think for a moment. But then I had it. "A large woman wearing fluttery clothes?"

"An excellent description. Her name's Myrtle Grabinowitz, and she's a dreadful gossip. Long story short, she mentioned meeting you to the Mekyles. As a result, they came to Indianapolis, to see what they could find, I expect. We thought we'd better come too and make sure you were safe."

"But I don't know them. Why would hearing my name induce them to come here, and how would they know about this house, anyway?"

"This is all conjecture, but we think when Agatha knew Stanley wouldn't live much longer, she decided to return the stolen art. Two men who had spent their careers locating stolen art were contacted as possible go-betweens. Norman was one of them. We suspect Malcolm was the other. Fortunately, or unfortunately, I suppose, depending on your point of view, we arrived first. That meant we were the ones charged with the return of the paintings. But although Malcolm arrived second and wasn't shown the collection, I'm guessing Agatha met with him and let slip information about us. He must have decided it was worth trying to find out what more we knew. In fact, we believe he and Thelma moved into Brookside in order to keep an eye on us."

"Why didn't they just break into the house earlier?" I said.

"They might have decided it was too risky. They probably didn't know your folks had died. Not to mention, there must have been an alarm system of some sort?"

"Not really." What I didn't say was that an alarm system wasn't really needed since most of the art was so well hidden. I thought about everything Josephine had said. "It all sounds so improbable."

"It is improbable but there's rather a large reward at stake. And money often makes people do improbable things."

"So, that's what they're after . . . what you're after? The reward?"

She shrugged. "I expect it's what they're after. But will you believe me if I tell you Norman and I have more money than we can ever possibly need? So, no, the reward isn't that much of an incentive for us, although the FBI thinks it is. What Norman and I are most interested in is getting the art returned to its proper place. And we would like it if the FBI no longer suspected us of forgery."

"Are you guilty?" It's Agatha's theory that hitting someone with an unexpected query leads to all kinds of useful information. Although, if that response isn't put into words, I'm likely to miss most of the information.

Josephine took a breath and looked me in the eye. "No, we aren't. But I understand why they suspect us. I would too, in their shoes. But the first we knew the painting wasn't genuine was when the museum's experts completed their tests."

"You said the other works are authentic?"

"In preliminary tests. I'm sure they're being retested. At any rate, we haven't heard further. At least, not yet."

I stared at her, trying to decide if what she was saying made logical sense. There were a few holes. The main one being her lack of interest in the reward money. Very few people have no interest in money. Although, actually, I don't.

But how did one prove such a thing, without turning over bank records? And even then . . . it does seem like some people can never have enough. Still, it was a question worth asking.

"Can you prove you have plenty of money?"

She frowned, obviously thinking about it. At least, she had the same kind of expression Agatha used to get whenever I asked her a question about my biological family.

"Okay," Josephine said, glancing at me. "There's this. I own an Edward Hopper painting. I expect you know his work now sells for millions. In fact, the last painting of his sold at auction brought in forty million."

I nodded. I'm well aware of the astronomical sums paintings like Hopper's command at auction.

"My painting, *Sea Watchers*, is currently on long-term loan to the Cincinnati Art Museum."

The information rang a faint bell in my memory. Didn't Devi say something about Josephine owning a painting?

"Upon my death, the painting will become the property of the museum. If I needed or wanted more money, I could simply sell it instead."

"Why not give them the painting now?"

She smiled and nodded. "Excellent question. You met Devi."

I decided it was a comment, not a question, and waited.

"I provide the art museum with a grant that pays Devi's salary. As part of her duties, she arranges for the painting to travel to other museums on short-term loans. If I donated the painting to the museum now, I might not have the same . . ." She stopped and shrugged, smiling at me. "Control. Over its movements."

I pulled out my phone and did a search on *Sea Watchers*. The first listing that appeared had the partial headline, "Cincinnati Arts Patron Josephine Bartlett . . ." I clicked the read-more link and found a news article about how one Josephine Bartlett had turned over the painting *Sea Watchers* to the Cincinnati Art Museum on a long-term loan with the promise the painting would be willed to the museum.

"It says Josephine Bartlett," I said.

"Right. I only recently married Norman. Until then, my last name was Bartlett."

That rang a bell as well. The real estate agent's prattling had covered the subject of a recent wedding.

I scrolled through the article to find a photo of two women next to a painting. I expanded the women's faces and recognized Josephine and Miriam O'Pinsky.

Although there wasn't much time left for waffling, I still wasn't ready to share any of the house's remaining secrets with the Neumans. Except maybe for one, which they apparently already knew about anyway.

"You said you saw Agatha and Stanley's collection?"

Josephine nodded.

Before I could say more, there was a knock on the door. We answered it to find Norman carrying a piece of glass and a bag of tools.

Josephine and I accompanied him to the back of the house and helped by handing him tools as he replaced the pane of glass in the back door.

"You need to change this to a double dead bolt, so that even if someone breaks the glass again, they won't be able to open the door. Or better yet, replace this door with a solid one."

"I'll let the executor know. He can arrange it." Then I pulled in a breath. "There is something else you can help me with."

"What's that?" Norman said.

"I'd like to check on the downstairs gallery. But I don't want to do it alone."

"Why don't the two of you go," Norman said. "One of us should stay up here in case there's any problem with the elevator. Or more unwelcome visitors."

I was glad he suggested it, as I agreed that it wasn't a good idea for the three of us to be in the elevator at the same time with no one else knowing that's where we were.

When Josephine and I reached the basement, it didn't take us long to check the area because there was nothing to see. Not a single painting remained. Even the picture hangers had been removed.

Since I knew at least ten paintings had been left behind after I removed the ones Agatha directed me to, it was obvious I wasn't the only one helping Agatha empty out the house. Although several missing rugs were also proof of that.

I suspected the helper had to be the man who'd come to live with Agatha and Stanley two years ago. That was when Agatha finally admitted that walking was difficult, and taking care of Stanley with part-time home-care aides had become impossible. Agatha had said the helper was a cousin, which I doubted. But then, I was learning I'd known very little about Agatha and Stanley. She'd also said he went back to England directly after Stanley's death, but I now doubted that.

For a moment, Josephine stared at the empty walls before the two of us returned to the elevator.

"There's nothing down there," Josephine told Norman when we reached the ground floor.

He didn't seem particularly disappointed at the news. "At least we don't have to worry there's anything here for Malcolm and Thelma to help themselves to," was his observation.

I almost said something then. About the figurine and the cardboard tube. But the moment passed.

"Is there anything else we can do to help you?" Josephine asked me.

And there it was. The perfect moment in which to solicit their help. "No. Nothing," I said, banishing it.

I was determined to check out what I'd found in the upstairs hiding place, but I wanted to do it by myself. I needed to get rid of the Neumans, then carry everything I found out to my car and take it to my condo, where I could examine the contents without involving anyone else. Even someone seemingly as trustworthy as Josephine, or Norman.

"You'll let us know if you need us?" Josephine said.

*The Babbling Brook Naked Poker Club – Book Four*

Again, I wavered before my decision to go it alone solidified.

# Chapter Twenty-Seven

## *Josephine*

When we left the Scott house, both Norman and I agreed there was something about Madeline's responses that was just . . . off. Did she really not know what had happened to the other art? But when we'd stepped out of the elevator into the basement, it was obvious she'd been expecting to see paintings, because I doubt she could have faked her surprise so convincingly otherwise.

"There's something about that girl," I told Norman as we climbed into our car.

I looked back at the house. Madeline had walked us to the door and waited there, at least until we reached the gate. I know because I'd turned to look back and had seen her. But now she was no longer standing there, and the door to the house was closed.

"She's socially awkward," Norman said. "Maybe because she was raised by such elderly parents."

"Yes, I expect that's the reason her word choices sound so formal."

"Actually, she sounds a lot like you, love."

"Better than sounding like a Myrtle. She's also very bright, you know. When I told her we had enough money, we weren't motivated by the reward, she asked me to prove it. So I told her about my painting, and she looked it up. After that, I thought for just a moment she was going to tell me something."

"About the paintings?"

"Who knows?"

"We know there were other paintings, though. And something's happened to them," Norman said. "As for the ones sent to us, Agatha couldn't possibly have done all of it herself. Packaging everything up, labeling it, mailing it."

"I can buy she addressed the labels, though. Myrtle was right. They were handwritten with a very shaky hand. But as for the rest . . . given Agatha was in a wheelchair, at the least, she'd have needed someone to drive her to the post office. And if that someone wasn't Madeline, how did she know the paintings were sent to us?"

"Good point. There's also the man who answered the door that day."

"Is there any way to check on him?" I watched as Norman negotiated the on-ramp to the interstate.

"We don't have a name. So that's looking like a dead end. I think our next step is to get back to Cincinnati and drop in on the Mekyles."

"Do you really expect them to go back to Brookside and act like nothing happened?"

"Why wouldn't they? I expect they'll simply act outraged if we accuse them of anything untoward. No doubt they'll say they found the window already broken and were concerned, like we were, about Madeline's safety."

"You mean Bernice?" I teased him.

"Unicorn."

Norman was probably right, and thinking about that, I put a hand on his arm. "I don't think we should go."

"What? You mean stay in Indianapolis?"

"Madeline's hiding something," I said. "And if it's the paintings, she's playing with fire. She could find herself in deep trouble. I want to help her."

"What are you suggesting?"

"Camping on her condo doorstep until she returns, and trying to make her see sense."

Norman appeared to be thinking about it. But then he shook his head. "It's best to leave her alone to work it out first. And meanwhile, maybe a visit with the Mekyles will prove useful."

# Chapter Twenty-Eight

## *Mac*

I stopped by to see Jo and Norman, both to assert my independence from FBI restrictions as well as to share the news of my impending change in status.

"Mac. Good to see you. We were going to call you," Norman said.

"About?"

"We're just back from Indianapolis. And do we have a story for you."

Norman poured me some of the excellent Scotch they keep on hand. I told them about my promotion, and then I heard about their ongoing Indianapolis adventures.

I thought through what they'd told me. "So your investigator found no evidence the Scotts had a daughter, but this woman showed up claiming to be their daughter? Given the extent of the Scotts' potential art fraud, she needs to be investigated."

"We have someone looking into her. As a matter of fact, he might have sent me an update by now." With that, Norman got up and left the room.

Jo frowned at me. "Could the Mekyles really get away with it? I mean, breaking into the Scotts' house and all?"

"If they didn't take anything, and you say there was nothing to take, there wouldn't be much interest on the part of law enforcement."

"Spoken precisely like a chief of police," Jo said.

"Sorry. You're right. Don't need to fall into bureaucratic-speak quite yet. Bottom line, though, even if Madeline Scott files a report, there's not much to go on."

Norman walked back into the room and handed both Jo and me pieces of paper.

"So, one thing we know with absolute certainty is they didn't adopt her," I said, skimming through the information.

"That means she's been lying about being their daughter," Jo said.

"Not necessarily," Norman said. "Her history with Stanley and Agatha goes back over twenty years. Although there's no evidence she was adopted, she lived with them from the time she was," he glanced down at the paper, "about four, I'd say."

"Curiouser and curiouser," Jo murmured.

I shook my head. "She can't be a complete fraud then. Not with a long-term relationship like that. Perhaps she's their granddaughter?"

"No. We've already verified Stanley and Agatha never had children."

"Maybe she's a niece or a grandniece."

"As far as the investigator could determine, both Stanley and Agatha were only children," Norman said.

"So, what we have is a mystery inside a mystery," Jo said, summarizing. "Although . . ." Her tone was thoughtful. "You have someone skilled in art restoration who's been raised by two people who, it appears, were art thieves and possibly forgers. She had to have figured that out at some point. And then either became an accomplice, or . . . maybe she's the one who talked Agatha into returning the paintings."

"Maybe," Norman said.

"I still can't figure out why she came to Cincinnati with the obvious intention of checking on us," Jo said.

"Well, if she was involved in the art's return, maybe she became concerned when there were no media reports about that return. And I can't say I blame her for that," Norman said.

"She asked us about that." Jo turned to me. "But if she knew about the art sent to us, how could she not know what happened to the other paintings we saw?"

"Did she say that?" I said. "That she didn't know?"

Jo's lips firmed. "We asked, but I don't remember getting an answer. But she was obviously surprised there were no paintings in the basement."

"There were quite a few paintings there four months ago." Norman's tone was equally pensive. "Maybe Agatha arranged with someone else to return them. And maybe that's what Madeline was getting ready to share with you." Then Norman turned to me. "Jo had the impression Madeline was debating about telling her something, and I have learned to trust Jo's impressions."

So had I, since they'd so far netted a couple of thieves and a murderer who, without Jo's intervention, would have gotten away with her crime. Although, Jo's crime-fighting successes have been due, up to now, to her partnering with Lillian Fitzel. But then, Norman has investigative skills of his own, which makes the two of them formidable foes of any lawbreakers crossing their path.

"I still think she didn't know that the other paintings had been removed by . . . who, do you suppose?"

"Possibly the butler did it." Norman's lips quirked.

"Yes, we keep forgetting about him," Jo said. "But then, we don't know his name, or his connection to Stanley and Agatha."

"I doubt he was an agency temp," Norman said.

"You realize there's a growing body of evidence that the elderly often make very questionable decisions about important aspects of their lives, and they are more easily scammed than younger people?" I said.

"I hope my son doesn't hear about that," Jo said. "But you're saying it's possible the man caring for Stanley might not have been trustworthy." She stopped and chewed on her lip. "We also need to remember they were ready to trust Malcolm Mekyle, had he arrived before us. Or that's what we suspect."

"We don't know that Malcolm isn't legit. He could be investigating this the same way I would have if I had the information he has."

"Would you have broken into the house?" Jo asked in a tart tone.

Norman's head wagged back and forth. "I don't know. With a stolen Rembrandt on the line, I sure would have been tempted. And didn't you tell me you considered breaking into Edna's apartment when you first suspected her of theft?"

Jo had the grace to blush. "Not break in. Just walk in, that is if she'd left her door unlocked."

"And did you?" I asked, trying to sound stern.

"No, I did not." Then she shrugged. "But only because Lill said she'd tattle to you about it."

That made me chuckle. "As a friend and a police officer, I'm glad to know you're restraining your criminal impulses."

"Can you please convince the FBI of that?" she said.

"Why not tell them about Madeline?" I said. "It will help clear you of suspicion entirely, and just maybe they can find out what happened to the rest of the art."

"We told them about Stanley and Agatha and gave them the address for the house," Jo said.

"But based on what we saw today, even if they got a search warrant, there was nothing there," Norman said. "Unless they were the ones who removed everything."

"I doubt they had enough evidence for a search warrant," I told them.

"Norman, you know that girl is going to need our help," Josephine said. "I think we need to get back to Indianapolis."

He sighed. "Maybe we could call Madeline before we rush off this time."

"Fine. Why don't I call her right now? You have her number, right?"

Norman gestured at the paper she was holding. "It's all there. Do your worst, love."

"I will."

She walked out of the room, and seconds later, I heard a door close and then the murmur of a voice.

# Chapter Twenty-Nine

## *Lillian*

Josephine called to tell me about the encounter she and Norman had with the Mekyles in Indianapolis. "Could you maybe check to see if they're back?"

"Oh, I know they are," I said. "I saw them walking in from the parking lot about an hour ago. You really think they broke into that house looking for more art?"

"I know they did."

"How did they even know to go there?"

"It's a long story. Let's have lunch soon, and I'll tell you all about it. But right now, I need to call Madeline. I think Norman and I will be going back to Indianapolis tomorrow."

Josephine ended the call, and thinking about the whole thing, I wandered over to my window, which overlooks the parking lot. There had been something odd about the Mekyles this afternoon. They'd looked . . . furtive? I shook my head, willing the memory to return.

And then I had it. Thelma had been carrying a long tube . . . like the ones Josephine had claimed contained curtain rods.

And Malcolm had been carrying something as well. A bundle of some sort clutched in his arms. Items stolen from the Scotts' house? Possibly. I started to smile. Myrtle wasn't the only one who could investigate a mystery. Not by a long shot.

This was going to be so much fun. Mac wouldn't approve, of course. But then Mac is paid to disapprove. Besides, he likes me. He probably wouldn't arrest me.

That thought about arrest gave me pause, but then I brushed it aside. This was important. Josephine and Norman had been under a cloud of suspicion for weeks. It was time somebody did something about it.

And let me just say if the Mekyles could break into someone else's home and steal something, it could hardly be considered a crime for me to steal it back.

Yes. There. The perfect comeback if Mac scolded me. It would be nice to have some help, though, and I knew just the person for that.

I hurried to catch Edna before she left her apartment for dinner.

"It would be a violation of my parole," she said when I explained what I wanted to do.

"Fiddlesticks. We'd be stealing from a thief, or two thieves, actually. I don't think that counts."

"Of course it counts," Edna snapped. But as I watched, a thoughtful look took over. "You know, you could be right about that. As long as we don't keep what we take. And . . . well, if they extend my community service, that wouldn't be all bad."

There it was. Confirmation Edna enjoyed her service.

I smiled to myself and waited a moment, to let her think about it, before saying, "I know this is the right thing to do." Of course, I didn't exactly know that, but I didn't dare appear hesitant or Edna would be out, and I needed her for my plan to work.

"But how do we do it? We can't just knock on the door and push our way in," Edna said. "We need for them to invite us in. How do we do that?"

I knew I'd hooked her. Now to reel her in. "We go to their place while they're out. If we wait a few more minutes for dinner to start, we can get a master key from the night meds guy."

"And how do we do that? Walk up to him and say, 'Hey, Brian, we're going to break into the Mekyles', and we need your key to do it?'"

"Not exactly. We tell him I locked myself out and I need to borrow the key."

"What if he insists on walking you to your door?"

"He won't. I've seen him getting the meds ready. It's quite complicated and requires close attention. Besides, you're going to come along and distract him."

"How do I do that? And what if he makes a mistake?"

"You're the criminal mastermind, Edna. You'll think of something."

Her lips pursed and then she got a calculating look. "Here, I have a better idea. You distract him, and I'll grab his key and go open the door while you keep on talking to him until I get back."

I had to think about that—how far the Mekyles' apartment was from the med staging area—down one short hall and then around the corner. I've seen Edna scooting along pretty fast when she needs to, so it was doable. And she was correct that Brian might not be willing to just hand over the master keycard if I asked. He might even say I needed to go to the office and have them let me in.

I was glad to see Edna was brainstorming, although brainstorms at our age are little more than brief sprinkles. Still, I was quite certain we'd figure out a way to finagle the keycard out of Brian's possession with him none the wiser.

Then I had an even better idea.

While the staff open doors as needed with keycards, we residents still have keys. They don't actually fit in a lock, though. They're like automobile keys, where you push a button. And I'd just remembered I had a key to Josephine's apartment. She'd given it to me when she was hospitalized after she was drugged. Or maybe it was after she was poisoned. Anyway, I'd used it to pick up some clothes for her, then forgotten to return it. I knew chances were excellent the lock had been changed when she moved out, but given the complexities of the system, and the expense of the keys, it might not have been.

I led Edna back to my place, past two residents on their way to dinner, and went to my desk. After digging around for the key, I found it and brandished it for her. "Let's see if this works."

"By this time, everyone should be at dinner," she said.

"I think we should knock first, to make sure they've gone. But we'll have to have a reason to be there, just in case."

Edna shrugged. "How about inviting them to a naked poker game?"

I wasn't certain they'd go for it, but then all we needed was a somewhat plausible excuse for knocking on their door. Hopefully, they wouldn't be there.

We waited another five minutes before venturing out. The hallway was deserted, as we'd waited long enough for the walker and wheelchair brigade to have made its way past. The parrot cage was still sitting outside Josephine's door, but it was covered. Which I took to be a sign Thelma and Malcolm had left for dinner.

I pushed the doorbell, and we waited. Then Edna reached past me and pushed it again. We looked at each other. She firmed her lips and nodded. I pressed the lock release on the key, and presto, we were in. It was almost too easy.

"How about we uncover the parrot," I said. "That way we'll be warned if they're coming. And you stand by the door while I look."

"Absolutely not. I'm not putting my good name in jeopardy to be nothing but a lookout, Lillian Fitzel. You uncover the parrot and stand by the door."

"You don't exactly have a good name. Besides, you have no idea what we're looking for."

"So tell me. Then I think we both should search. It will go twice as fast."

"Oh, okay. We're looking for a green tube. And a bundle about the size of a football, I think."

"Dibs on the bedroom," Edna said.

With an annoyed humph—after all, this was *my* idea—I glanced around the living room, then proceeded to the den where I found the tube sitting propped against the desk.

*Bingo.*

And only fair that I should be the one to find it.

I pulled the end off and felt inside. Nothing. Well, that was annoying. I gave the room another look before heading to the dining room. And there on the table was a painting. Its edges were weighed down, because otherwise it would have curled up. It had to be what was in the tube. I examined it while I waited for Edna to rejoin me.

She stuck her head in, then caught her breath and walked over. "It's old, isn't it?"

"I believe so." I removed one of the items weighing down a corner and turned the edge of the canvas over so I could see the weave. I remembered from my reading that modern canvas, produced by machines, has a very tight and even appearance.

This canvas was yellowed and the weave was uneven. I could be wrong, but I judged it to be old. How old, I had no idea.

The painting was quite nice. A windmill scene with muted colors and a single area of brightness. I could barely make out a letter or two of the artist's name. R-u-i-s . . . something, something, I decided.

"Did you find anything?" I asked Edna.

"I think so."

"Well, show me, then we need to get going."

She led me into the bedroom, and there, sitting on the floor, was a peculiar-looking figurine. "It was under the bed."

"I don't think we can take the picture without them noticing, but we could take this. I'm sure it's what Malcolm was carrying."

Edna had to help me lift the figure. But once I was standing, I was okay with the weight. "Let's get back to my place," I told her.

"You're sure that's what Malcolm was carrying?"

Of course I wasn't completely sure. But that was a minor quibble. An attempt had been made to hide it. That was good enough for me.

Back at my place, I set the figure on my table and had a good look. "I think it looks Egyptian, don't you?"

"M-maybe we'd better return it."

I looked at my clock. "Oh, we can't. Dinner will be over soon."

"Well, as far as I'm concerned, I never went near the Mekyles'," Edna said with a sniff.

"Neither one of us did, Edna. If the matter comes up, we just stumbled across this in a flower bed."

"You stumbled across it."

I gave Edna one of the looks that used to cause small children to stop fidgeting and sit up straight. "Fine accomplice you make, Edna Prisant. With your experience, I expected better of you."

After Edna left, I took a closer look at the figurine. I'm no expert, but it looked just like a picture in one of the books about art fraud I'd read. That made me a little nervous. But, after all, there was no way for the Mekyles to know I'd taken it. Unless . . .

I swallowed, and suddenly I couldn't have eaten a bite, even if a plate of food was right in front of me. Josephine had installed video cameras. Of course, she'd taken them with her, but what if the Mekyles had installed cameras of their own?

I fought the urge to stuff the figurine under my bed. Instead, I placed it on my bookshelf. Hiding in plain sight . . . more or less.

I realized I'd have to confess what I'd done to Josephine and Norman, and the thought made me even more nervous. Whatever had come over me to do such a thing?

I sat down abruptly and clenched my hands to stop them shaking. What was done was done. I'd just have to live with it. Like Edna lived with her wrongdoings. But I'd do it with a hat on my head and an upward tilt of my chin.

Oh my.

# *Chapter Thirty*

## *Maddie*

When I got back to my condo, I got out scissors and worked on the tape closures on the cardboard tubes I'd found in the hiding place in my old room. Carefully, I removed canvas after canvas, laying out each in turn, hoping one would be the missing Rembrandt.

I opened the last tube, examined its contents, and sat back, discouraged. No Rembrandt.

I went back through the paintings, examining each more closely. Three of them were canvases I'd seen Stanley copy. I couldn't tell whether these were originals or his copies. I knew the canvases were old enough, but it would require an expert with specialized equipment to examine the pigments.

Three of the paintings were ones I'd not known were part of Stanley's collection. They were question marks of a different type. I recognized them from my art history classes, and when I checked the art database, I found them all listed as "current location unknown."

I added up the estimated worth of the paintings scattered around my living room. If they were originals, they were worth at least seventy million. A number that made me gulp. Did Agatha know about them, or had they been hidden from her as well as the world? Or maybe she knew but forgot? I shrugged in frustration. There was no way to find out now.

As I finished looking at the paintings, the phone rang. Josephine Neuman was calling. Reluctantly, I answered.

"Madeline, I just thought you should know. We had to tell the FBI about Agatha and Stanley. I apologize . . . we tried to keep our promise to Agatha. We understand that she didn't want the return of the paintings linked to her. But with the discovery that the Rembrandt was forged, we didn't have a lot of options."

The news made me gasp, and it took me a moment to recover. "When was this? That you told them, I mean?"

"About five days ago."

"Well, they haven't come." I think I must have sounded impatient. This whole stolen/forged art thing was wearing on me.

"My dear, I know you don't have any reason to trust us any more than I trust the Mekyles, but . . . I think you know something about the missing art, and it won't take much of a leap for the FBI to think that as well. And if you do have some idea where the other paintings are, maybe the Rembrandt is there too."

"No, I already checked." I wanted to smack myself, but I couldn't recall the words. I pressed a hand to my forehead and squeezed.

"Did Agatha tell you that some of their paintings were stolen and needed to be returned?"

"Y-yes. But . . . there's a problem." I hesitated, then feeling like I was stepping into an abyss, I spoke the next fateful words. "Some of the art is probably authentic, but Agatha didn't know which was which. If I return fakes, that's going to cause one kind of problem, and if I return originals, the people who thought they purchased those originals . . . well, they might come after me."

"We can help you."

"How?"

"For starters, we can be with you when you call the FBI art fraud unit."

"I don't know if that's a good idea. This whole thing . . . it's such a . . . m-mess." It was a relief to admit it to someone, even if I couldn't manage it coherently.

After a brief silence, Josephine spoke again. "I really want to help, but I think you're still suspicious of me."

Her uncertainty steadied me, getting me back on track. "I am. Because there's been no announcement about the return of the Elizabeth Kent Oakes art. I know you said you returned it, but that doesn't mean you did."

"Of course. I understand your hesitation. Why don't I have the museum director call and verify for you that it's in their possession. Would that help?"

Again, she paused, and I had no idea how to answer. Except she was correct. If I knew for sure the art had been returned, it would probably help. "Y-yes, I'd like that."

"Okay, I'll arrange it. After that, if you agree, Norman and I will come, and together we'll talk to the FBI. We already know two of the agents pretty well."

"I . . . I have to think."

"I understand how difficult this is. Especially since Norman and I have gone through something similar already. But I can't advocate for you either concealing the art or delaying any further its return."

Although I hesitated to respond, deep down I knew that what she was saying was the right way to go about it.

"I do have one important question, Madeline," she said, pulling my attention back from its meanderings. "Do you know if the Mekyles took anything from the house?"

I sucked in a quick breath.

"They did, didn't they," Josephine said.

I let the breath out. She already knew most of it; why not admit the rest? "There was a painting . . . I saw it on my way upstairs, and when I came down to answer the door, when you knocked, it wasn't there. So they probably took it."

"Do you know which painting it was?"

"I barely glanced at it. It was hanging in the corner, and the lighting wasn't very good. It was one of those dark portraits."

I was lying, or at least dancing around the truth, but if I mentioned the figurine, it would lead to other questions. Agatha always said the best defense was a strong offense.

"I'd like that proof you returned the art." I spoke firmly, as if I were the one with the upper hand. "Then I'll decide what to do."

Although, having already admitted to Josephine that I had more of Stanley and Agatha's collection in my possession, my choices had narrowed. I would no longer be able to hide and deny indefinitely.

~ ~ ~

I went to bed feeling frustrated and very alone with the problem Agatha had left me.

In the morning, the phone rang early, waking me from a restless night. The call was from a man who claimed to be Gerald Huntington, the director of the Elizabeth Kent Oakes Museum. He verified that Norman and Josephine had indeed returned the paintings.

When I asked him to prove he was who he said he was, he first directed me to the museum's website, then told me to call the main number that was listed there and ask to be connected to the director. When I did that, I was connected to him. If he'd faked the call, it was an excellent fake.

Now I had to choose who to trust.

## Chapter Thirty-One

### *Josephine*

Norman and I got up early. After we took our usual walk, breakfast seemed like a good idea, but I found I was too twitchy to eat much.

"How long do we need to wait before talking to the Mekyles?" I said.

Norman glanced at the clock. "It's nearly eight. We can go now."

"Shouldn't I call Madeline first?"

"Let's talk to the Mekyles first and then call Madeline. Maybe by that time, she will have spoken with Huntington."

I was in a fever of impatience to confront the Mekyles and be done with it, but Norman thought additional witnesses were a good idea, so I contacted Lill and Edna, who said they'd be happy to join us. When we met in the lobby, both were acting a bit oddly, I thought. If I had to label it, I'd say they were nervous. But perhaps they were just excited to be included. After all, Lill knew what I suspected the Mekyles of.

The four of us walked the familiar route to my old apartment in the GloryDove wing. The parrot started muttering as soon as it spotted Norman, and I moved quickly to cover it up. It let out one loud squawk, then subsided.

When Norman knocked on the Mekyles' door, Malcolm opened it and frowned at us. "Why are you here?" His tone was unfriendly to the point of being aggressive.

It pushed my buttons, and I opened my mouth to say something I'd no doubt regret. I felt a hand on my arm and turned to find Lill shaking her head at me. I let out a breath, nodded at her, and she released me. It had been a gentler reminder than the kicks under the table she usually employed.

"We're here to speak to you and Thelma. To compare notes on our recent visits to Indianapolis," Norman said.

Malcolm bristled and stood on his toes, in order, I expect, to be eye to eye with Norman. I figured he was working up to telling us to go away, but then he stepped aside so we could file in. He called out to Thelma.

She bustled in from the bedroom, then hesitated when she saw all of us. "What's this about? A naked poker game invitation, perhaps?"

"Excellent guess, but no cigar," Lill said. She had obviously grasped the gist of my hurried explanations.

"We're here on Madeline Scott's behalf to ask you to return the painting you removed from the Scott house when you broke in yesterday," Norman said in a perfectly pleasant tone of voice.

"I have no idea what you're talking about," Malcolm blustered, but Thelma put up a hand to cut him off.

"We found the front door unlocked," she said. "We were just taking a look to make sure nothing was amiss." Her tone communicated that she knew we couldn't prove otherwise. "As for this painting you're referring to, perhaps you mean the *curtain rod* box we discovered on the stairs?"

"Perhaps we are. Would you be willing to share?"

"Of course. Unlike some people." Her smile was as unpleasant as her tone.

She led us into the dining room where a painting lay stretched on the table. I noticed Lill giving Edna a nudge, and then the two exchanged a look of . . . relief?

Thelma gestured with a flourish at the painting. It pictured a windmill standing against a dark sky. A single beam of light came through a break in the clouds and drew the eye to a small figure.

I looked up to see both Thelma and Malcolm glaring at Norman, who was bent over the painting. He carefully fingered one edge, turning it to examine the back of the canvas.

"I see what you mean," he said, straightening.

"What?" Both Lill and I spoke simultaneously.

"It looks like van Ruisdael's work. It's certainly his kind of sky, but it's not quite right."

"A forgery, you mean?" Edna said, her tone eager.

"People do copy the old masters. It's not a crime unless they try to pass it off as an original." Norman frowned. "It's quite good. And I could be wrong about it being a copy."

"You aren't," Thelma said.

Madeline had said the missing painting was hanging on the wall, in a dark corner. "So, where's the frame?" I said.

"Frame?" Thelma gave me a puzzled look that appeared genuine.

"The one you took this painting out of."

"The painting was in a tube when we found it."

"And where exactly did you find it?"

She shrugged. "I told you. On the stairs. We thought it was odd that it was just sitting there."

Madeline said she'd noticed the painting hanging in the corner near the stairs, which made the Mekyles' account sound even more peculiar. "Did you talk to Madeline while you were in the house?"

"You're talking about Madeline Scott?"

I nodded.

"As far as we could tell, there was no one in the house."

At least that part jibed with what Madeline had told us. "You don't deny the painting belongs to Madeline?" I said, staring at Thelma and Malcolm.

"All we know is that it was in the house. We were acting on a tip that the house contained stolen art. Obviously, it didn't. She's welcome to it. We apologize for the misunderstanding." Malcolm's tone was unctuous.

Norman, like me, must have decided it wouldn't gain us much to ask him what "tip" he was referring to.

"I'd like to see the tube it was in," Norman said.

Thelma huffed but then left the room, returning a moment later carrying a long tube that she thrust into my hands while Norman rerolled the painting. The Mekyles had smug expressions, which I found odd, but with Norman moving toward the door with the painting in hand, I didn't have time to explore the thought further.

"So nice of you to stop by," Thelma said. "Anytime you'd like to get together for a game, just let us know, won't you?"

The door closed behind us.

"Can we come to your place, Lill?" I asked. "There's something I have to tell you."

"Do you mind if I come too?" Edna asked.

"Not at all." We were close enough to the end, I didn't think including her was a problem. Besides, she isn't a gossip, and she'd been willing at a moment's notice to help us this morning.

As soon as we were inside Lill's apartment, with the door closed, I told them what Madeline had said about the painting, concluding with, "Bottom line, either she's lying or the Mekyles are."

"Somehow, I suspect Madeline's the one twisting the facts here," Norman said. "I doubt the Mekyles keep copies of what appear to be old masters on hand, just in case someone accuses them of stealing something. And it is rather a good copy."

"We need to go back to Indianapolis."

Norman nodded. "I expect that's best. Confronting Madeline over the phone won't have quite the same power as showing up on her doorstep with the painting."

"You two have the most exciting life," Edna said, sounding pensive.

"Only if you consider boomeranging between Cincinnati and Indianapolis to be full of drama and excitement," I said.

Lill cleared her throat. "There's something I need—I mean, that Edna and I need—to tell you."

Norman, in the midst of fitting the painting back into the tube, stopped, and we both gave Lill and Edna our attention.

"We sort of," Lill said, "kind of—"

"We broke into the Mekyles' apartment last night," Edna said with a quick glance at Lill.

"You what?" Norman said.

Lill plopped into a nearby chair. "I know, I know. It was stupid. But after you called and said you'd seen them in the Scotts' house, and I saw them walking in from the parking lot carrying that tube—"

"And something else," Edna said, interjecting.

"Yes. Malcolm was carrying a bundle, and we just thought it might be helpful if we . . ." Lillian stopped speaking and pointed at an item on her bookshelf.

With a quick inhalation, Norman stepped closer. "You found this in the Mekyles' apartment?"

"Under the bed," Edna said.

There was a knock on the door, and after exchanging panicked glances, Lill went to answer.

"Well, am I glad to see you're all right, Lillian." The fruity tones could belong to only one person. Myrtle Grabinowitz. "When you weren't at breakfast, I just thought it best if I checked, and . . . oh, hello, Edna. Josephine?" She peered further. "Oh, and Norman. How nice to see all of you."

We were busted. Norman slid sideways until he was blocking Myrtle's view of the peculiar figurine.

"I'm fine, Myrtle," Lill said. "We're all fine. We're going out to brunch to celebrate . . . ah . . . um . . ."

"We're celebrating Edna's successful completion of her parole," I said.

Edna blinked but said nothing. Lill's shoulders looked less rigid.

"Oh, well, I do think you could have included me. I am Edna's best friend, after all."

I glanced at Edna in time to see her roll her eyes.

"You're right," Lill said. "But this is just a quick brunch. Spur of the moment. But Josephine and Norman are going to have a party, and you'll be at the top of the guest list."

"A party. How nice. You'll be sure to serve those mini quiche thingies, won't you, Josephine?"

I needed to cut this off before Lill made any more rash promises. "Norman just got a call, and we need to get going. I'm sorry, Lill, Edna, we'll have to do the brunch another time."

"Oh. Well, I'm sorry too," Lill said. She shrugged at Myrtle, who finally took the hint and backed reluctantly away from the door. Lill closed it and slumped, blowing out a breath. "That woman . . ." She shook her head.

"So now I have to have a party . . . with mini quiches, no less?" I said.

Norman started to laugh, and then we all did. When we'd caught our breath, Lill asked what to do about the figurine.

"Let's just leave it here for the time being," was Norman's advice. "Although, you need to be aware it could be quite valuable."

"H-how valuable?" Lill asked.

"Enough to bump a misdemeanor breaking-and-entering up to a felony." Norman looked stern, and Lill wilted further.

"Guess I'm not cut out for the life of a criminal," she muttered.

"If it's that valuable, I think we should turn it over to Mac," I said.

"Oh yes. Let's do that."

"And you're going to tell him you have it because . . ." Norman said.

"I'll tell him the truth."

"Which is?" I said.

"I was walking by the Mekyles and noticed their door was open, and I just worried that they'd forgotten to close it and—"

"Fine. You take care of calling Mac. Norman and I are going to Indianapolis."

"I used your key," Lill said. "I just forgot you didn't live there anymore." Her expression dared me to contradict her.

"And when you visit me, you're in the habit of looking under my bed?" I gave Lill a stern look, and she looked steadily back. If it hadn't been for a twinkle in her eye, I might have been a little worried about her, since she was always the one who insisted we stay on the straight and narrow when we were investigating Edna.

"Call Mac. Now. And don't let anyone else in. Especially if their name is Mekyle."

"I promise," Lill said.

~ ~ ~

I wanted to let Madeline know we were coming back to Indianapolis, but Norman said the element of surprise was important. Madeline could very well be playing us, he insisted, and confronting her with the painting might clarify matters.

I also wanted to call Mac before we left, but Norman argued that Lill needed to take responsibility for her actions.

"I think she felt bad that Myrtle got to help, and she didn't," I said.

"I doubt Mac will be too hard on her."

"Probably not. But still . . ."

"We need to get going, Jo. We can worry about Lill and her criminal activities after we talk to Maddie."

Reluctantly, I agreed.

Snow was in the morning forecast, but we encountered only light flurries. In the outskirts of Indianapolis, the snow stopped, but there was still a heavy overcast. Madeline answered her door and ushered us in. Without surprise, I might add.

"I was hoping you'd come back. I need your help."

"That's why we're here," I said. "What do you need us to do?"

Norman was carrying the tube containing the painting, and Madeline's eyes widened when she spotted it. "Where did you get that?"

"From the Mekyles," I said. "Do you know what it contains?"

She shook her head. "I'm guessing a painting, but I don't know for sure."

"Why don't I show you?" Norman pulled off the top and slid the painting out. Then he stepped over to a table and laid it out flat.

While he did that, I watched Madeline's reaction.

When Norman stepped aside to reveal the painting, her hands came up to cover her mouth, and she drew in a quick, sharp breath. If she was faking her surprise, she was extremely good at it.

"Do you recognize this?" Norman asked.

Madeline nodded. She stepped closer and took the edge of the painting between two fingers, rolling the canvas between them, then she turned over the top right corner. "Yes, I'm very familiar with this painting. See this mark here?" She pointed to a tiny dot. "I made this mark after I painted it. When I was sixteen."

Her expression dared us to comment.

"You're very talented," I said. "It's a fine painting."

"An excellent copy," Norman said. "But I don't believe an authenticator would be fooled for long."

"No, I expect not. I had trouble with the colors, so I used some of my paints instead of Stanley's pigments. He was quite disappointed."

"The Mekyles said they found the painting in this tube, lying on the stairs," I said.

"That's correct."

"You told me the missing painting had been hanging on the wall."

"I didn't trust you."

"Why was the painting on the stairs?" Norman asked.

She pulled in a breath and looked away. Then she looked back at us. "It's a long story. Maybe we should sit down?"

We settled in her living room. The walls were painted a dark blue that contrasted with the oatmeal color of the carpet, couch, and two chairs. Attractive, but with no photographs or knickknacks scattered about, it had a model-apartment vibe.

"I guess it's best if I start at the beginning," Madeline said, joining us. "Stanley and Agatha weren't my parents, but they raised me. I think maybe I was the daughter of a friend of Agatha's, but she'd never tell me for sure. Stanley taught me to draw and paint from an early age. That painting," she nodded toward the windmill painting lying on the table, "was the only copy I painted."

"But Stanley was a forger?" Norman said.

Madeline nodded. "In a class of his own. After I painted that," she gestured toward the painting again, "I rebelled and refused to do any more. And I started painting whatever I wanted to."

"And you became a restorer."

"By that time, I had a lot of experience dealing with old canvases. And I was much happier restoring paintings than trying to copy them."

"You were talented, though," Norman said. "What gives that painting away isn't the brushstrokes and subject matter, it's the pigment hues."

"I did that on purpose, actually. By the time I painted that, I had a pretty good idea what Stanley was doing, and . . . well . . ."

"We get it," I told Madeline.

She nodded. "Thank you. So, anyway, after I got back from Cincinnati, it occurred to me I might know where the Rembrandt was. So I contacted the executor, and he gave me the key to the house. When I got there, I began checking Stanley's hiding places. I located the painting and a figurine in one of the hiding places and left them sitting on the stairs while I went up to my bedroom. And that's when the Mekyles arrived. They knocked first, and when I didn't answer the door, they broke in. I hid until I thought they were gone. Then you arrived."

Her story, although concise, was so multifaceted, it took time for me to put all the pieces together.

Norman managed that more quickly. "There was a figurine along with the painting, you say? Can you describe it?"

Madeline did so, and Norman smiled at me. "Sounds like the item Lill took from the Mekyles."

"It does, indeed," I said. "And it's no wonder the Mekyles acted smug when they realized we were only after the painting. I wonder what they'll do when they discover it's gone."

"Panic, maybe?" I realized Madeline was looking at us as if we'd sprouted second heads. "We know where the figurine is," I told her. "It's in very good hands. A friend of ours stole it back from the Mekyles."

Madeline sat back, blinking. "That's good, right?"

"Very good. Serves them right." Thinking further, I added, "They'll hardly be in a position to press charges against Lill."

"About the other paintings," Norman said, returning to the most important point. "Are they here?"

Madeline nodded. "What should I do about them?"

"We need to contact the FBI fine art retrieval unit as soon as possible. But, meanwhile . . . I'd love to see what you have."

It took over an hour for Madeline to unroll each painting and for Norman to look his fill. Among the paintings, we found what appeared to be the original of the windmill painting.

Norman and Madeline bent their heads over each painting in turn, examining them closely and discussing their findings. Finally, the last painting had been examined and returned to its tube.

"I've been thinking," Norman said. "About the hiding places in the house. How many are there?"

"Three. One in the conservatory, a second behind the stairs, and the third in my bedroom."

"Is it possible there are more?"

Madeline's expression registered uncertainty, then excitement. "You know, there could be more."

"How difficult were they to find?" Norman asked.

"The three I know about are all concealed behind carved paneling."

"Is there carved paneling in other rooms?"

She paused, then said, "Stanley's studio . . . there's a fireplace similar to the one in my room. And there are carved areas in at least two other bedrooms."

"You still have the key?" Norman said.

Madeline nodded. "I'll get it." She jumped up and practically ran from the room.

Norman gave me a look, a mixture of excitement and anticipation.

Madeline returned brandishing an ordinary-looking key. Somehow it seemed all wrong for a house with as much gravitas as the Scotts' mansion.

~ ~ ~

The heavy overcast rendered the winter sun invisible. And inside the house, the light was dim. Madeline turned on the lights. I glanced up to see a chandelier, whose elegance was more than a match for the carved staircase.

"Let me show you the places I know about," Madeline said. "It might give you a hint about what we're searching for."

After Madeline pointed out the area behind the stairs as being where the release for the first hiding place was located, I asked her to let me see if I could find it. I ran my fingers over the carvings. If there was a seam somewhere, it was hidden perfectly. Tentatively, I pushed and pulled on several of the more prominent parts of the carving. Then I stood back and examined the entire area. Possibly I needed to go lower, since Madeline discovered this spot when she was seven. I ran my fingers over a full-blown rose. Abruptly, with a barely perceptible click, part of the paneling moved.

"Hey, you're good at this," Madeline said.

"It helped that you told me roughly where it was," I said, straightening.

"The second hiding place in the conservatory is similar, so why don't I show you the one in my bedroom?"

We followed her upstairs.

"Don't tell me where it is," I said, examining the elaborate fireplace surround. Then I decided that with the amount of carving, it might take a while. "You can tell me which side."

She pointed to the left side.

I ran my fingers over the carvings in the area she'd indicated. Then I knocked to see if I could locate the hiding place, but the entire area gave back the same solid thump. I was about to give up when I noticed a lone bunch of grapes partially obscured by leaves in the design. I tapped the cluster of grapes. Nothing. Then I placed my fingers on them and twisted in a clockwise direction. Again, nothing. I tried again, twisting counter-clockwise. And with that, I was in.

"Wow," Madeline said. "I didn't discover that until I'd spent over a decade living in this room."

"No way I'd have found it if you hadn't told me where to look. So, what was in here?"

"The paintings I showed you."

"These might be only the beginning of what could be here," Norman said.

"That's true. And the most logical location for another hiding place is Stanley's studio. Come on, I'll show you."

She led the way up a second flight of stairs, this one much more sparsely decorated than the stairs between the first and second floor. At the top, we entered a large open area. Skylights made the most of the weak winter light, and Madeline added more light by pulling a string attached to a utility-sized bulb hanging in the center of the room.

Although the light it gave off was bright, the edges of the room remained in shadow. Within the bright as well as the shadowed areas sat easels, some with canvases propped on them. Small tables next to the easels sported palettes, tubes of paint, and dried-out brushes in glass jars that no doubt at one time held paint thinner. Also present were some tins of the type that hold varnish. I picked one up, and something inside sloshed.

Norman made a beeline to the corner of the room where canvases were stacked, while Madeline stepped over to the nearest easel to examine the partially completed canvas.

My attention was drawn to the fireplace. Oddly, its position was roughly opposite the fireplace in Madeline's room. I turned and saw a brick chimney where I expected to see it, based on the position of the fireplace below us. Gazing back at this room's fireplace, I wondered if it was merely ornamental, although it was more simply carved than the one in Madeline's room. It also had an unfinished aspect, as if the carpenter was on a break and would shortly return to do a final sanding before the entire piece was given a second coat of varnish.

I approached the fireplace, and this time when I ran my finger over the carving, I encountered rough areas. None of them seemed to hide a mechanism, however. I continued to run my fingers over the surround, tapping and then twisting the upraised bits in the carved areas. Nothing.

Frustrated, I stepped back and studied the fireplace as a whole. There was an irregularity in the otherwise symmetrical design above the mantel. I placed my finger there and tapped.

A panel above the fireplace swung out. When I gasped, both Norman and Madeline rushed over. Within the aperture that had been concealed by the panel hung a painting.

Norman held up his phone, using the flashlight feature to illuminate our find.

I felt like I should fall to my knees, but my knees aren't what they used to be, and the floor was bare wood. Glancing at Norman and Madeline, I could see the same awe in their expressions that I was feeling.

We'd found the missing Rembrandt.

# Chapter Thirty-Two

## *Maddie*

As Norman, Josephine, and I stared at the painting hanging in the recess, I heard a faint ringing and knocking. Someone was at the front door.

"Do you think I need to answer that?" I said, gesturing toward the stairs, hoping they'd say no.

"We've turned on a lot of lights, in a house that's been empty for a while. Probably just a neighbor checking. We'll shut things down here and be right behind you," Norman said.

I glanced at the painting, and Norman nodded.

Reassured, I hurried down the stairs. The pounding on the door grew more insistent as I approached, and it was reassuring to know Norman and Josephine had my back.

I opened the door. "Can I help you?" My heart rate, already elevated from running down the stairs, bumped up further when I saw two policemen were standing there.

"Yes, miss. Just a routine check. Can you provide identification?"

"I'll have to get my purse, but I'm Madeline Scott, the daughter of the owners, Agatha and Stanley Scott."

"If you would get your purse, we'd like to verify that."

"Just a moment." I pulled the door mostly closed and looked around. Norman and Josephine were remaining out of sight, thank goodness. I retrieved my purse from where I'd dropped it by the hall closet and took it back to the front door, where I presented my driver's license to one of the officers.

"You don't live here," the officer said after looking at the license. "Why are you here today?"

"I'm picking up some things I left behind when I moved."

"What things?" said the second officer. His tone made me feel six years old, awaiting punishment for misbehaving.

"I'm a painter." I simply couldn't manage nuances at the moment. "I left several of my canvases here. I came to pick them up." It was close enough to the truth that I didn't have a problem sounding convincing. At least, I hoped I didn't. I firmed my lips, trying not to let any more words escape.

"And your parents. Where are they?"

For a beat, the question bewildered me. Then I realized I had the perfect answer. "They're in Colorado." Which was the literal truth since I scattered their ashes there before returning to Indianapolis.

The officer holding my license handed it back after taking a picture of it with his phone. "All right, miss. Neighbors noticed the lights, thought we should check. Thank you for your time."

I started to sag with relief before realizing it would make me look guilty of . . . something. I straightened instead. "Thank you for your concern." I had no idea where the words came from, but they sounded exactly like something Agatha would say.

~ ~ ~

As soon as the door closed on the officers, Norman and Josephine appeared on the staircase.

"Is everything okay?" Josephine said.

"I think so."

"We left the lights on, so it wouldn't seem odd . . . lights going off while you were at the door," she said.

"That's good." I was slowly recovering from my fright. My heart was no longer madly pounding, but I was shaking all over.

"We need to decide what to do about the painting," Norman said. "My advice is to leave it where it is and contact the FBI."

"We've closed it in again. To keep it safe," Josephine said.

"That's good." I had to stop speaking to clench my teeth together to keep them from chattering. So, not totally recovered yet.

"Are you two up to checking for more hiding places?" Norman asked.

Although I couldn't seem to stop shaking, I knew this might be my last chance to be in the house.

We went from room to room, searching carefully, knocking and tapping, but we found no other bits of carving that opened to cavities in the walls.

"I guess that's it, then," Norman said after we'd examined all of the bedrooms, paying special attention to the fireplaces.

In a way, I was thankful to be done searching for more paintings. I already had a sufficient number to worry about. I did a final check of the stack of paintings on the third floor and found no other lost masters among them. Some of them were old, however, and I suspected Stanley was planning to use the canvases. This jibed with the paintings on the easels, which all appeared to be in various stages of having the original paint removed. But the thick layer of dust on everything indicated that nobody had been up here in months, perhaps years.

Stanley had started having difficulties with stairs about three years ago. Since the elevator only connected the ground floor and the basement, it's probable that was when he was last up here.

Several of my early attempts to paint something original were in the stacked pile, and I pulled them out. "I'd like to take these with me," I told Josephine and Norman.

"That shouldn't be a problem," Norman said.

"They're quite good," was Josephine's comment. "Do you still paint?"

I shook my head.

"You should," Josephine said. "This one . . . it's special." She reached for one of the paintings, walked over and set it on the nearest easel, and then stood examining it. It was one I'd forgotten I'd painted. Seeing it now, I recalled the morning I'd awakened with an image in my mind as sharp and detailed as one of Stanley's favorite paintings.

I'd jumped out of bed, and without stopping to change out of my pajamas, helped myself to a new canvas and began painting. It felt at times as though my hand was being guided. When Agatha came to call me for school, she'd seen what I was doing and left me to it.

The product of that intense inspiration was a painting of a young girl of five or six, in profile, standing in a stubbled wheat field that stretched to the horizon, facing a woman, also in profile. The girl was dressed in an old-fashioned coat and bonnet and was lifting a small basket toward the woman. The girl's expression, only partially visible, was solemn. The woman wore a translucent white dress and a blue cape, like a Gothic heroine. Her expression, although only partially visible because of her cloud of dark hair, was likewise serious.

Remembering the intensity of the urge to paint this particular picture, I was surprised I'd forgotten it so completely. I was glad to have it back.

~ ~ ~

After I got back to my condo, I remembered one other hiding place I hadn't checked. I'd forgotten it, I suppose, because we were hunting for paintings, and this particular hiding place was too small for that. It was one Stanley had shown me when I was six, a place he and I then used to share secret messages.

I don't know if Agatha ever knew about our game, and I don't remember when or why it ended. Possibly when I got older, I decided it was a baby's game.

I was tempted to return to the house right then. But it was a forty-five-minute drive. And if neighbors saw lights going back on, they might call the police. Again. Resigned to a possibly sleepless night, I decided it was best to wait until morning.

The morning dawned with clear skies, but with an inch of snow on the ground. Knowing I had to return the key soon and that I'd be meeting later with Josephine and Norman to arrange our call to the FBI, I dressed and, skipping breakfast, returned to the house. The hiding place Stanley and I had used was a simpler affair than the others. There was no elaborate carving to manipulate and no well-oiled panel to pop silently open. All this hiding place required was the sideways slide of the third stair riser.

With held breath, I slid the panel open and used my phone to shine a light inside. The cavity held an envelope, its thickness indicating it contained several pages. I pulled it out. Underneath lay one of my childish drawings with a printed message on the back. Perhaps it was the last note I left Stanley. So maybe he'd been the one who discontinued the game.

I retrieved the drawing, closed the panel, and stuffed the envelope and drawing into my shoulder bag. Then I stood there next to the stairs, and for a time did what I'd told the executor I wanted to do—remembered Stanley and Agatha and grieved their loss.

It had been a gift, no matter that Stanley was a criminal, for me to have been part of their lives.

~ ~ ~

When I returned the key to the executor, I mentioned the broken glass in the back door. "I fixed it, but you need to install a better lock or different door."

"I suppose you're right. Although there should be nothing left in the house for them to steal."

"Yes, I noticed."

"Were the things you wanted still there?"

"Oh. Yes. My paintings. They hadn't been touched, as far as I could tell."

"Good. I wasn't entirely comfortable with your mother's instructions about the house."

"Why not?"

"I was told to provide authorization, should there be any questions from neighbors or police, for a Leonardo Vincent to oversee the removal of certain furnishings from the house."

"When did she tell you to do that?"

"Shortly before the two of you left for Colorado."

Maybe that explained why she hadn't wanted me to return to the house. Although had she told me those were the arrangements she'd made, I'd not have objected. It was her house and it contained her things, after all. I was glad that the mysterious Leonardo had left the paintings on the third floor untouched, however. And that he'd not known about the hiding places.

"But who was he, this Leonardo Vincent?" I asked. "Did you meet him?"

"No. We talked on the phone, and when he let me know he'd completed the task, I arranged for the locks to be changed."

"Did he have an English accent?"

"He did. Rather like your mother's. Perhaps a relation?"

He had to be talking about the man who'd been caring for Stanley the past two years. When I visited, he'd always promptly removed himself from any room I entered.

"Neither Agatha nor Stanley ever mentioned family," I told the executor. Then I had a thought. "Do you have a way of getting in touch with Mr. Vincent?"

"I have a phone number, but the last time I called, it was out of service."

"Could I have it anyway?"

He buzzed his assistant and asked her for the file. "You don't think anything improper occurred, do you?" he asked me.

"No, of course not. Agatha was sharp as a tack to practically the last day. If it was her wish that Mr. Vincent clear out the house, I have no reason to question that." I realized abruptly I'd painted myself into a corner. What reason could I now give for wanting Mr. Vincent's out-of-service phone number? I steadied my breathing. "I'd just like to thank him personally, if possible . . . maybe the phone will come back on. He saved me a lot of work and worry."

"Yes, of course. I can see that."

The assistant knocked, then came in and handed the executor a file. The executor opened it and glanced through several pages before picking up a pen.

"There are two numbers here. I'll give you both." He wrote the numbers down and handed me the piece of paper.

I accepted it, then shook his hand. I doubted I'd ever need to see him again.

"Good luck, Madeline. Your parents were extraordinary people, you know. It was my honor to serve them."

It was an odd statement on which to end our meager association. I nodded in reply.

Later, I tried the numbers. Both were out of service, which meant the mysterious Leonardo would remain mysterious. But since that appeared to be Agatha's wish, I tamped down my curiosity. I had many things to do, and none of them required me to meet with, or talk to, the peculiarly named Leonardo D. Vincent.

# Chapter Thirty-Three

## *Lillian*

Josephine called when she and Norman got back from Indianapolis for the third, or maybe it was the fourth, time. I confess I've lost track. Boomeranging was the perfect word for it.

"What happened with Mac," was Josephine's first question.

"He wants to speak with you," I said.

"I'm not surprised. And we want to speak with him. Actually, we have quite a tale to share. With him and also with Devi and Edna. We don't require black tie, but we won't discourage it either." I could tell from her tone, Josephine was grinning.

Despite thinking she was mostly teasing, I dressed up anyway. Ever since I started wearing my church hats again, I've looked for opportunities to give them an outing. And it was especially important to keep up appearances now since Mac had not been happy with me.

It meant this situation called for as much flamboyance as I could manage. I decided on the fuchsia hat, which is still as much in style as the day I bought it thirty years ago. And it will force me to keep my head up, even if I am feeling ashamed of myself.

A good thing I resisted my daughters' suggestions to donate my church clothes to Goodwill. Goodwill, indeed. Better I give my hats and dresses an occasional outing than hand them over to some woman who'd let her grandchild play dress-up with them.

Josephine gave my hat an approving look.

"Lill, you are definitely going to have to take Jo hat shopping," Norman said.

"I don't think so," Josephine said. "You do realize it takes years of practice to carry off a hat like that?"

"That may be," I told Josephine. "But you aren't going to get started any younger. And with appropriate tutoring and practice, I believe I could have you wearing a hat by Easter. *Mm-hmm.* Looking fine."

Devi smiled. "I really want to see that."

"And I, for one, believe Lillian when she says she can help you change," Edna said.

I thought from the way they were teasing me, I'd been forgiven. At least, I hoped so.

"Maybe we could find a hat for Devi too," Josephine said, sliding a glance over at Devi.

"I'd like to see that," Mac said, winking at me and putting an arm around Devi. That wink was the final straw, lightening my load of guilt.

"Enough about hats," I said. "We're all dressed up, drinking champagne, and eating with our fingers, and I know there's got to be a good reason for that."

Josephine and Norman shared a glance full of affection and mischief.

"We are celebrating the return of not only the missing Elizabeth Kent Oakes art, but of eleven additional paintings," Norman announced.

"Does that include the Rembrandt?" Devi said.

"It does."

I clapped my hands, Devi and Mac beamed, and Norman and Josephine looked proprietary. Edna was the only one who looked slightly at sea.

"And the person who discovered where the Rembrandt was hidden is right here." Norman turned and raised his glass to Josephine. "To Jo. Another mystery solved."

"And this time I wasn't poisoned or drugged," she said, smiling at Norman.

"A situation for which I am profoundly grateful," Mac said.

"And I wasn't the bad guy this time," Edna said, obviously catching up to what was going on, and clearly forgetting our little caper.

"So, do we get to hear everything?" Devi said.

"You do. It's rather a long story, so perhaps you'd all better help yourself to appetizers and get comfortable. Norman, you'll be on glass-refilling duty?"

"Of course."

Josephine began her account with the arrival of the art in the mail nearly five months ago. She and Norman then took turns, filling in the parts we didn't all know, and I have to admit, it made for a gripping account.

I wished I'd been able to play more than a bit part, although to be fair, I'm not a big fan of road trips. I glanced at Devi, and guessed from her expression and the way she was fingering her still full glass of champagne, she was thinking the same thing. About being part of the investigation, not the part about all the travel.

But our reward for what little help we had provided was that we got to hear the complete story. And we were the only ones who would, because Norman, Josephine, and Madeline had made a deal with the FBI. In return for turning over the rest of the art, along with detailed information about Stanley's activities, the involvement of Madeline and the two of them in the art's return would not be shared with the media.

There was only one little thread still dangling when they finished.

Josephine turned to Mac. "Your turn to tell us what happened with the Mekyles."

"Ah, yes. Thelma, Malcolm, and I had a most productive conversation," Mac said. "Turns out Mekyle was Thelma's maiden name. Malcolm's real last name is Johanssen, and he's an art investigator, like Norman."

"Not exactly like Norman." Josephine's words held a snap.

Mac nodded. "No, not exactly like Norman. I did encounter an unexpected difficulty in speaking with them." He tipped his head, giving me a look. "The figurine Madeline told you they'd taken from the house was no longer in their possession."

"An Egyptian bronze," Norman said. "Worth a great deal of money. We don't know what Stanley was doing with it since his weakness appeared to be paintings."

"The Johanssen-Mekyles claimed they had no knowledge of it, because . . ." Mac stopped and looked right at me. "I believe this is your part of the story, Lill."

"Yes, well, I guess all of you know by now, I wanted to help. And I saw Malcolm carrying a very suspicious package, and well . . ."

"You went to their apartment when they were out and helped yourself. Right, Lill?" Mac said, sounding stern.

Edna cleared her throat. "Y-you didn't tell him I helped you?"

"Of course not. And why would you want to horn in on my bit of glory. I mean, it might not have been completely legal, but it saved the figurine from being carried off by the Mekyles and possibly lost."

"Not completely legal?" Mac raised his eyebrows. "It's lucky for you the Mekyles have no idea you were the one, excuse me, *ones*, who took it. And also lucky they were forced to deny they'd ever been in possession of the figurine."

"What about the painting?" Josephine asked. "Clearly, they removed that from the house."

"They claim they found evidence of a break-in and just wanted to check there was no one in the house. They picked up the painting by mistake, after Josephine and Norman rang the doorbell and panicked them."

"As a former thief, I have to say I don't buy that," Edna said with a skeptical lift of her brow.

"Neither did I," Mac said. "Even though they were extremely courteous, not to mention sincerely regretful they'd removed the painting 'by mistake.'" He bracketed the last words with air quotes.

"Were they also regretful they'd sought to mislead us with an alias?" Josephine's eyebrow arched.

"I don't believe so." Mac appeared to be trying to suppress a chuckle.

"Well, did you arrest them?" I asked.

Mac shook his head. "I didn't arrest you, did I? I had even fewer grounds for arresting the Mekyles."

"And where is the figurine now?" Devi said.

"Safe in the vault at the Cincinnati Art Museum, until its provenance can be determined."

"If it turns out Stanley didn't steal it, which I expect is unlikely, it will be a nice nest egg for Maddie," Josephine said.

"Don't forget, Maddie already has a nice nest egg," Norman said with a grin. "Stanley's business model appears to have been to copy paintings he'd arranged to have stolen, then he sold the copies to unscrupulous collectors, who are in no position to come crying for their money back."

"But wouldn't that mean her inheritance falls into the category of ill-gotten gains?" Devi said. "I mean, the FBI could simply consider it the result of a criminal enterprise and confiscate it all."

"True," Norman said. "But don't forget, Maddie's an innocent in all of this. That means she's also eligible to collect any rewards in the offing for the return of the paintings. And those will be substantial. She's going to be a very wealthy young woman."

Which, in my opinion, was the perfect outcome.

## Chapter Thirty-Four

### *Josephine*

Norman and I were at dinner in the Brookside dining room when Myrtle came at us.

"Toodle-oo, you two," she chirped. "And Lillian, of course." She grabbed a seat and fluttered into place. "You're just who I was hoping to see. And don't you dare try to tell me ever again those packages were curtain rods, Josephine Bartlett. Because I know better."

I knew it was useless to argue with what Myrtle thought she knew. But it also seemed like the curtain rod issue should be behind us by now. Besides, Myrtle's theories weren't relevant, as the FBI no longer suspected Norman and me of any crimes.

"It was very clever of you to see through it," I told her. "But we'd promised to keep it all a secret, you see."

"You could have trusted me. I don't believe I've ever betrayed a confidence."

This blatant disregard for the facts left Norman smothering a laugh with his napkin, and Lill and me with open mouths.

Myrtle didn't notice our reactions as she was busy looking around the room. "Oh, there's Edna. We really should include her, don't you think?"

"Include her in what?" I asked.

"Why, the celebration, of course," Myrtle said, waving a hand at Edna, who we'd already arranged to join us.

As Edna walked over, Myrtle summoned one of the servers and gave her the task of squeezing in a fifth place at the table.

"I imagine Edna will find this news especially titillating," Myrtle said. Then with a ta-da motion, she pulled a copy of *USA Today* out of her tote bag. "Just try to tell me you didn't have something to do with this, Josephine."

The headline was *Empty Frames Filled with Long-lost Masterpieces*. A photo of the missing Rembrandt, back in its proper place on the wall of the Elizabeth Kent Oakes Museum in Boston, accompanied the article. And further in, there was a photo of the da Vinci drawing Myrtle had glimpsed on my dining room table at the start of everything.

"You see this? Right here. This picture. I saw this. You know I did." She prodded the paper and then nodded her head in satisfaction. "And I'll bet neither of you had a clue our Josephine, and Norman, of course, were involved in something so, so dangerous and exciting. A ring of international art thieves, no less." Her free hand clattered into place over her heart.

"Not a clue," Lill said, rolling her eyes at me when Myrtle wasn't looking.

"All I can say is I'm very happy I was able to help the FBI with their inquiries and had at least a tiny part in this," Myrtle said. "And I'm not one bit fooled by this article. This reporter doesn't know what she's talking about."

"Why do you say that?" Edna said. "I thought it was all pretty straightforward."

"Well, it doesn't mention Josephine and Norman, does it? Or Madeline Scott."

"Of course it doesn't," I said, feeling the tiniest spark of annoyance. Norman and I had almost twisted ourselves into pretzels to avoid being mentioned. As had Madeline.

"Anonymous return, my aunt Fanny. You have to tell us the real story, Josephine."

"Only if I lose at naked poker." I was immediately sorry I'd been flippant, because Myrtle jumped on it, of course.

"What an excellent suggestion. Tomorrow? Two o'clock? I'm sure I can find people to join us."

Lill's lips went through several contortions before they stopped twitching.

As I tried to come up with an excuse, Myrtle frowned. "Too bad the Mekyles won't be able to join us. I tell you, that whole thing was extremely odd." She shook her head.

"What was?" Norman said.

"Why, that policeman friend of yours, Josephine. He and another policeman came to see the Mekyles, and the next thing we knew, their things were being moved out and their apartment was being painted. If I didn't know better, I'd suspect they were arrested."

"How do you know better?" I said.

"What?"

"You said if you didn't know better . . ."

"Oh, that. Well, just the other day, while you were away," she nodded toward Norman and me, "I had a conversation with Thelma, and she told me they'd come into a sudden inheritance, and it meant they could afford to move back to New York. You see, they found it was much too expensive to live there once they retired. That's why they came to Cincinnati. But now with the inheritance, they must have gone back. Although, moving in the middle of winter doesn't seem like such a good idea. And, of course, they could've said good-bye to me. After all, I did introduce them around and make sure they got to know people."

"I agree. Most ungracious of them." I slid my glance over to Norman, who avoided looking at me. I suspect if he had caught my eye, he would have been unable to smother a chuckle.

~ ~ ~

"You'll be extremely lucky if Myrtle doesn't call the newspaper with a scoop that totally blows your cover," Lill told us as we walked her and Edna back to their apartments after dinner.

"Would anybody listen to her?" I said.

Lill shrugged. "They might not want to listen, but we can all attest that Myrtle's hard to ignore. She's like a freight train. Once she heads down the track, there's no stopping her."

"Well, we all have a stake in trying to make sure she's diverted onto another track," Norman said.

"I'll do my best," Lill said with a sigh.

"As will I," Edna added.

We bid Lill and Edna good night and walked hand in hand back to our home.

A few flakes of snow spiraled through the wash of light by our front door. The air was crisp and the night still. And for at least the next five minutes, I was not going to worry about reporters or the possibility of angry art collectors showing up on our doorstep.

# Chapter Thirty-Five

## Maddie

As I left my condo for a last run to the bank, I passed a satellite news truck. I slowed and watched in my rearview mirror as it parked on the street across from my place.

Norman had warned me that even though we could trust the FBI to keep their agreement with us, it didn't mean that some enterprising reporter wouldn't dig further. We'd been collectively referred to as an anonymous tip in the announcement about the Elizabeth Kent Oakes' art return, which was the only return that had so far been reported. But still . . .

Norman's reasoning, which the satellite truck verified was impeccable, was that once the FBI searched Agatha and Stanley's property, something they insisted was necessary since not every stolen painting in the known universe had been recovered, the news media would get wind of it, and the chase to find Agatha, Stanley, and anyone associated with them would be on.

"It might be a good idea for you to leave for a while," Norman said.

"Why don't you come to Cincinnati?" Josephine said. "Stay with us. Then we'll figure out the next step. I already have a couple of ideas about that."

I decided to take her up on her suggestion. My intention, when I returned from the bank and before I spotted the news van, had been to pack the car, then get a good night's sleep before leaving for Cincinnati in the morning.

But knowing a news van was lying in wait, I altered that plan. Instead of returning to the condo after the stop at the bank, I drove until I reached the interstate and headed east.

I made it to Cincinnati in four hours, driving under overcast wintry skies with blowing snow half the way, and in misty darkness, with even heavier snow, the remaining half. I pulled into Josephine and Norman's driveway at eight.

When I knocked, Josephine opened the door and, seeing me, smiled an Agatha sort of smile. "Maddie, I'm so relieved you're here. Come in."

"Sorry, I wasn't thinking clearly. I should have let you know I was coming tonight."

"It's okay. We're just glad you're here. We were so worried when we saw the news report and then you didn't answer your phone."

"News report?"

"Yes. Norman has a news alert on his computer. Anytime there's a new story about lost paintings, or something of that sort, it dings. It's been quite noisy lately. And this evening, there was a report on the CBS evening news about you."

"What did it say?"

"The reporter was outside your condo, and she said that you're Agatha and Stanley Scotts' daughter, and since the FBI search of your parents' property for missing art, you've been mysteriously missing as well. They even had a picture of you from your high school yearbook."

"I saw them arrive. I panicked and drove directly here."

By this time, Josephine had taken me by the hand and led me to a seat in the living room, and Norman had joined us. I was shivering. I didn't know if it was because I wasn't wearing a coat, and for the few moments I'd waited on their porch I'd gotten a chill, or if it was something more fundamental. Like the fear that some unhappy, mob-connected art collector might now be on my trail.

Josephine pulled an afghan off the back of a nearby chair and placed it around my shoulders. "You look tired."

I just nodded.

"Did you bring your things?"

"No. I'd packed . . . but I hadn't loaded the car yet."

"No problem. All you'll need tonight is a toothbrush and something to sleep in, and we have both of those. Tomorrow, I'll call Devi and we'll go shopping. Have you eaten lately?"

"I had lunch . . ."

"That had to be hours ago. How about some hot chocolate? And maybe a toasted cheese sandwich?"

"I . . . I guess so."

Josephine continued to sit with me, but she must have signaled Norman, because he left the room and headed toward the kitchen. "It's going to be all right," she said while we waited for Norman.

"I'm not so sure." I fought the urge to cry.

"The news media isn't going to be interested in this for very long. I swear, they have the attention span of a cloud of gnats."

I nodded. "And are just about as annoying." With the afghan around my shoulders, I was beginning to feel both warm and a little sleepy.

Norman returned with a plate and a mug. "Hope cheddar cheese is okay? And here's your hot chocolate."

"I'll get your room ready." Josephine patted me on the arm and left me with Norman.

They seemed to be playing tag team with me. But to tell the truth, I was glad.

Norman sat back and sipped his own drink, which definitely wasn't hot chocolate. It looked like bourbon, or maybe Scotch.

I found I was starving and made short work of the sandwich. Then I sat sipping the hot chocolate. "You were right. That they'd find me," I told him. "So, what comes next?"

"Right now, you finish that and relax. We'll talk about the future tomorrow, when we're all rested."

Ordinarily, I'd say I was perfectly capable of making all my own decisions, thank you very much. But I had asked him for help, and it was a relief to know both he and Josephine were willing to provide it.

## Chapter Thirty-Six

### *Josephine*

After Maddie's hectic departure from Indianapolis, she slept until nearly noon that first morning, and I left her to it. From her appearance the night before, I suspected she hadn't slept much for at least the last few harried days since we'd called the FBI to report that we'd found the missing Rembrandt.

Norman and I had stayed in Indianapolis to give Maddie support while the investigation wrapped up. I confess, being at the beck and call of the FBI had been wearing on us all. But those extra days in Indianapolis had given us a chance to become better acquainted with Maddie, as she'd asked us to call her.

When the FBI searched the Scotts' house, none of us volunteered any information about possible hiding places. So, who knows? Despite our careful search, and the FBI's, there might still be paintings hidden there.

The FBI brought in a team to recover the Rembrandt, which we'd left propped against the wall with the other paintings in Stanley's third floor studio. One of the neighbors shared a video with a local news reporter of agents walking out of the Scotts' house carrying paintings, and when that activity was quickly followed by the announcement that the Elizabeth Kent Oakes art had been recently recovered from an Indiana property, an astute reporter realized there might be a connection to the Scotts. And that led her to Maddie. It was a leap of conjecture similar to the one Myrtle had taken, but with better technology, in the form of a microphone and a satellite feed, to back it up.

By the time Maddie was up and dressed her first day on the run, Devi had arrived. Since it was a Saturday, she'd left Mac in charge of the twins. I watched Devi and Maddie chatting while I cooked Maddie French toast for breakfast, and it gave me a warm feeling to see my two favorite young women laughing with each other.

I suggested Nordstrom's for our shopping trip, but after a quick glance at Maddie, Devi suggested TJ Maxx and Old Navy instead.

"I know, why don't the two of you go shopping, and I'll drop in on Mac and help with the twins. I've been sadly remiss in my attentions to them lately."

"You have," Devi said, looking serious before beginning to grin.

I was home by four, and Devi and Maddie returned from their shopping trip shortly after that. They had many bags, both large and small, which they unloaded from Devi's car, laughing and chatting the whole time.

"I took the opportunity to buy a few things too," Devi told me.

"If you're going to be the chief of police's wife, you do have standards to uphold."

Maddie turned to Devi. "Ch-chief of police? I thought you said he was a cop."

"Sorry. It's a recent change." Devi turned to me. "I talked Maddie into moving in with us until she can find a place of her own. I hope that's okay with you?"

Since it had been one of my ideas, the other being she could stay at Norman's house, it was very okay.

The doorbell rang, and I answered it while Devi and Maddie pulled out some of their favorite purchases to model for me.

Myrtle stood on my porch. I swear, the woman has either developed psychic powers or has somehow enhanced her talent for being in the wrong place at the right time.

"Myrtle, what a surprise."

"I expect it is. I want to know why a car with an Indiana license plate is sitting in your driveway?" She pushed past me into the house. "Aha. I knew it. Madeline Scott, as I live and breathe."

Standing behind Myrtle, I shook my head in resignation.

"Curtain rods, indeed, Josephine Bartlett. I knew it was all going to fit together eventually. You aren't the only one who can solve a mystery."

The doorbell rang a second time, and I opened the door to find Lill. Behind her, Philippa's husband was driving away.

"I'm sorry, Josephine. I tried to stop her," Lill whispered.

I'd taken Lill with me to Devi and Mac's to play with the twins. She's as crazy about those babies as I am. And as we drove to Devi's, I'd told her the rest of Maddie's story, and that she was staying with us.

Both Devi and Maddie were frozen in place, staring at Myrtle, who looked like a Cossack in a voluminous red cape.

"Why don't we all have a seat?" Myrtle swirled the cape off her shoulders and passed it to Lill, who turned around and dumped it on the floor.

Myrtle was too deep into queen mode to notice. She sat in my favorite chair and smoothed her dress. Then she gave all of us a satisfied glance. "I'm waiting."

When none of us either spoke or took a seat, she firmed her lips. "Either you start talking, or I share everything I know with that reporter who's looking for you, Madeline Scott." She tipped her head.

"Snooty poodle crossed with pit bull," Lill whispered, then louder, she said, "You'd better tell her, Josephine."

I noticed Norman hovering in the doorway. When I glanced at him, he scooted out of sight. *Coward.* He was going to hear about this . . . later.

I shoved a couple of the shopping bags out of the way so Lill and I could sit down. "Devi, why don't you and Maddie move the fashion show to the bedroom."

With a quick nod, Devi scooped up several bags. Maddie followed suit, and the two left the room.

"Now, Myrtle, of course we're happy to tell you everything. But first you have to promise you won't be talking to any reporters. And I mean *any*."

"If I promise that, who's to say you'll tell me everything?" Myrtle said.

"Once you hear what we have to say, I believe you'll be moved by Christian compassion not to share it with another soul." At least, I hoped she would be. "Maddie is in a very difficult and possibly dangerous situation. And those of us who know her carry a heavy responsibility to make sure she remains safe. And that means absolutely no talking to reporters. In fact, it would be an excellent idea not to share it with anyone else, period."

I paused. It hadn't been difficult to sound serious since I considered this a very serious situation.

"Are you prepared to take a vow of silence, Myrtle?"

She sat back, her jowls quivering. "Well, I'd need to know what I have to be silent about before I could possibly promise such a thing."

"If you don't promise, we won't tell you anything," I said.

"If you don't tell me what's going on, I'll call that reporter," Myrtle replied. "She'll figure it out."

I bit my lip to keep the words, *You have no idea what you're toying with here, woman,* from escaping. At that moment, Norman entered the room. I suspected he'd been eavesdropping.

"Hello, Myrtle. You're not trying to blackmail my wife, are you?"

"Oh no, of course not." Myrtle giggled in a distinctly nervous manner.

"Good. I've always considered you an honorable person. I'd hate to think you'd do such a thing."

"Oh, I am honorable." Myrtle batted her eyelashes at him. "I wouldn't dream of blackmailing Josephine. Not at all."

"That's good to know." Norman smiled at Myrtle and took a seat in the other chair. "And since you're honorable, and you've guessed part of the story, you deserve to know the rest."

If he'd been closer, I would have kicked him. He should know by now that whatever happened in Myrtle, definitely didn't stay in Myrtle.

"Let me fill in the missing pieces," Norman said, ignoring my glare. "You guessed correctly that some missing art was mailed to Jo and me. And the person who mailed it was Agatha Scott. She addressed those labels that you surmised were not done by a computer. Her husband, Stanley, had acquired that art, illegally, many years ago. Agatha didn't even know Stanley then, so she was an innocent party. As is their daughter, Madeline.

"Stanley was a master forger. Something Agatha also knew nothing about until recently. She thought Stanley made copies of the great masters for his own amusement. She didn't realize that he copied original paintings he'd arranged to have stolen, and then sold those copies to other collectors. It meant that returning the art carried a . . . risk. Collectors who've purchased what they thought were original masterworks could discover that they'd actually bought worthless copies. That could make any number of unsavory characters very angry indeed."

As Norman continued to speak, I relaxed. I had a pretty good idea by that point that he intended to leave the really juicy bits out of his narrative.

"Before she died, Agatha enlisted our help in seeing that the art was returned, and that Madeline was kept safe. So, we are responsible for Maddie's safety, and now that you know what happened, you're going to have to join us in keeping her presence here a secret as well."

"Oh, I will. I will. They can pull out my fingernails, and I won't say a word."

"I doubt it will come to that." I realized when Lill tapped my foot with hers, that I'd sounded tart. But, honestly, Myrtle is one of the most annoying people I have the misfortune to know.

"I'm so glad to hear you say that." Norman's tone was the one that grates on my nerves.

Not that he uses it on me. He discovered its less-than-soothing effect the first time he did, and he hasn't tried it since. But from the way Myrtle was simpering—there's simply no other word for what she was doing—I could tell it had worked on her.

"Jo, would you and Lill mind making us some tea? It will give Myrtle a chance to get to know Maddie."

I stiffened, but then I caught Norman's glance. His expression was his please-trust-me-on-this one. And since, over the time I've known him, he has given me so many reasons to trust him, I led Lill from the room.

When we returned with the pot, cups, and a heaping plate of cookies, both Devi and Maddie were chatting with Myrtle.

"It's kind of amazing," Devi said. "Coincidences. Myrtle has a granddaughter named Madeline Scott."

"Yes, amazing. Cookie, Myrtle?"

"Don't mind if I do. I do love these shortbread ones. Don't you, Madeline?"

Maddie looked at me, and I had the distinct impression she was begging for help.

"Here, Maddie, why don't you try one?" Myrtle said, then veered onto another subject, one we could all get on board with. The twins.

Once the cookies and tea had been consumed, Norman offered to take Myrtle and Lill back to the main building. While Myrtle recovered her cape, with a snort of dismay at the way it was lying crumpled in my front hall, I whispered to Norman that I'd invited Lill to dinner.

"Trust me," he whispered in return.

"Norman has a plan," I told Lill as I got her coat out of the closet.

And he did. He returned fifteen minutes later . . . with Lill.

"He dropped me off at the front door and picked me up at the back," she said with a chortle.

"Excellent. Now we just have to call Mac to join us."

# Chapter Thirty-Seven

## *Maddie*

It took time to absorb everything in the letter from Stanley I'd found in the hiding place on the stairs. And once I did, I knew it wasn't something I'd ever share. Stanley must have placed it there when his illness forced him to give up painting, and shortly after that, walking. It was an extraordinary last testament of the most personal sort. Something that finally made sense of most of what I'd experienced and observed living with him and Agatha over the years.

Stanley admitted to being a thief and a forger. This was no surprise to me, as both the evidence in the house and my knowledge of his activities had already led me to draw those conclusions. But if the letter was to be believed, that wasn't the complete story.

Stanley had also been a confidential informant for the FBI. Throughout the past twenty years, they'd brought him original paintings to copy. These copies were subsequently used in sting operations to identify and ultimately prosecute unscrupulous collectors, and to recover some of the art they had obtained illegally.

*I would like to think I have had a role in returning many irreplaceable works to their rightful places and in protecting other works from being stolen*, Stanley had written. Of course, he'd also played a role in removing from view a number of irreplaceable works, including the eight paintings and drawings stolen from the Elizabeth Kent Oakes Museum.

I came by the Boston paintings purely by chance, he wrote. And then I was stuck. For who would believe I hadn't stolen them in the first place?

I felt frustrated that even as a final testament, Stanley was unwilling to give more details about how he acquired the art. I'd read all the press accounts, of course. Investigators suspected that mobsters had hired the three physically fit thieves who had disabled the alarm system, overcome the night guards, and made off with the art in an operation lasting about fifteen minutes. The guards didn't see faces, and the museum had no video cameras at that time.

The Stanley I knew had been, until his final illness, stout and physically inactive. I doubted that at the age of fifty, which is what he was at the time of the robbery, he could possibly have been one of the actual thieves. So how he "acquired the art by chance" would remain a mystery.

He did admit that before and after he acquired the Elizabeth Kent Oakes art, he'd stolen other paintings, always from collectors he considered dubious. He then made copies and sold the copies to other collectors he identified as being willing to deal in stolen art. He held on to the originals for his own pleasure, he said. Until the day he was caught mid-theft by the FBI.

He'd subsequently agreed to work with them in exchange for his freedom. When one of the sting operations led to Stanley being compromised, the FBI had placed him in witness protection in Indianapolis. There he met and married Agatha.

He didn't do a very good job of explaining why, once he was in cahoots with the FBI, he didn't turn over all the stolen paintings, including the ones from the Boston museum. Possibly that lack of a coherent explanation was the result of old age, or maybe it was embarrassment.

He closed by telling me I had been the light of his life, and that his only regret was that he was too old to live long enough to see me happily married. An old-fashioned sentiment . . . probably brought on by his advanced age.

In total, it was a convoluted, fantastical tale, one I would have had difficulty believing if I hadn't lived through a part of it. It was also frustrating since, like Agatha's last communications with me, it failed to clear up the mystery of who I was and how I'd come to live with them.

~ ~ ~

Thank goodness that by the time I'd been in Cincinnati ten days, the media had moved on from speculating about the return of the stolen art to other stories, and Norman agreed it was safe for me to make a quick trip to Indianapolis. I wanted to pick up my things and put my condo on the market.

And there was one other task I'd set myself.

Josephine and I had talked on several occasions about the paintings of mine that I'd rediscovered when we searched the house. In particular, Josephine wanted to know more about the one of the girl in the wheat field.

"That painting is one I could live with," she told me.

I think she was telling me something more. It was a conclusion based on the crash course in human communication I was embarked upon. Not just from Devi and Mac, but also from Toby and Lily, who couldn't even talk yet, but who were teaching me how to know what they wanted and needed without words.

I think Josephine was telling me she wanted that painting. And there's a perfect spot for her to hang it, in her living room. I remarked once on her bare wall, and she'd said, yes, she and Norman were waiting until they found the perfect painting to hang there, one they both loved, and that they preferred a blank wall to hanging something inferior.

On a whim, I'd asked her, "Do you consider my painting inferior?"

"I consider it anything but inferior."

I hope she meant it, because one of the main reasons I returned to Indianapolis was to retrieve that painting so I could give it to her.

Back in Cincinnati, before I turned it over to the framer, I'd shown it to Devi, and she'd gasped, then grinned at me. "So this is the painting Josephine has been raving about. I can see why."

"Do you think . . . I mean, does she really like it . . . or is she just saying that?"

As my communication lessons had continued, I'd learned that often people say things they don't really believe, in order to avoid hurting someone's feelings. I suspected that covered most of Josephine's communications with Myrtle. But I hoped Devi understood my need for absolute honesty.

"She told me about the painting when you weren't around. That absolutely means she loves it."

I got that now. That one person could say something about a second person to a third person, and those utterances were likely to be the truth. Or something of the sort.

"I . . . I want to give it to her. To thank her for all she's done. That's not a terrible idea, is it?"

"Wow. Not terrible at all. Perfect, I'd say. After all, Josephine's added you to her family."

"Oh . . . I didn't know. I mean, who else . . ."

"Who else does that include? Let's see . . . Lillian, maybe Edna, Mac, me, and Lily and Toby. And Norman, of course. And now you."

"Not Myrtle?"

Devi laughed. "I suppose she might consider Myrtle a distant, very annoying cousin."

"And being part of Josephine's family . . . what do I have to do?"

"It's simple. Include her in your life."

~ ~ ~

It took three weeks to get the painting back from the framer. I'd gone to the museum to see what kind of frame Josephine had chosen for *Sea Watchers*, and picked a similarly simple frame for my painting. I felt really, really nervous about giving it to Josephine, though. Mac figured that out, but then he was a detective before he became the police chief. And I expect once a detective, always a detective.

The day I got the painting back, I was having dinner with him and Devi. She left the room to finish getting the food ready, while Mac and I kept an eye on the twins.

"What's up with you?" Mac asked.

"How could you tell?" I said.

"Your leg is jiggling."

"I'm nervous."

"About your interview?"

I'd been offered an interview at the Cincinnati Art Museum. One of their restorers was retiring shortly, and Devi had let Miriam know I might be available. It hadn't occurred to me to be nervous about that, though. "Should I be?"

"Not unless you want to be," Mac said. "So it's something else?"

"Better if I show you."

I jumped up and hurried into the main part of the house where I'd left the painting propped by the back door. I unwrapped it and carried it back to Devi and Mac's suite. When I showed it to Mac, he whistled.

At the sound, Devi came out of the kitchen, wiping her hands on a dishtowel. "Oh, that frame is perfect."

"So, what are you nervous about?" Mac asked me.

"I want to give it to Josephine. Do you think she'll like it?"

Devi stepped closer. "It's extraordinary. I see why Josephine raved about it."

"I don't know much about art," Mac said. "But I could live with that painting."

Devi swatted at him with the towel. Lily came toddling over, and I had to lift the painting away from sticky fingers. Mac swooped in and picked her up, making her giggle.

"So, when are we doing this?" Mac said.

"What?" Devi said.

"Maddie's nervous, so I'm thinking we could drive her over to Jo's after dinner. And stick around. To witness the presentation, of course."

"We could fit that in, I suppose," Devi said.

"Put you out of your misery," Mac said.

"I'll give Josephine a call and warn her we're stopping by," Devi said. "And I'll call Lillian and Edna too, if that's okay? The whole family should be there for this."

"But what if she doesn't like it?"

"Tell you what," Mac said. "How about I give Norman a call. Check on the plan."

"An excellent idea," Devi said.

I sat, both feet jiggling now, listening as Mac talked to Norman.

"I need to ask you something, in strictest confidence, of course," Mac said after the usual hellos and how-are-yous were completed. He signaled for me to sit next to him, and held the phone out so I could hear Norman.

"Of course. What is it?"

"Can Jo hear you?"

After a rustling and then the sound of a door closing, Norman said, "Not now, she can't."

"Good. I need to ask you a tricky question. I need to know if Jo would welcome the gift of one of the paintings Maddie painted?"

There was a silence that seemed to stretch for about a week.

"Jo was impressed, but . . ."

My heart stuttered. I should have trusted my original hesitation. It was a stupid idea. I never could figure out what people really thought or wanted.

"You see, she was planning to ask Maddie if she could purchase that painting. The one of the girl."

"So if Maddie gave it to her, Jo would be pleased?"

"She'd be ecstatic. But it does put me in a bind."

"Why?"

"Since I knew Jo coveted that painting, I was hoping Maddie would sell it to me to give Jo for her birthday. So this sets me back to square one gift-wise."

"You'll cope, though?"

"Of course I'll cope."

"Do the two of you have plans for later this evening?"

"I suspect we do now."

"About eight okay with you?"

"Sounds good."

"Tell Jo we plan to stop by, just don't mention why."

"Can do."

Mac clicked off the phone and gave me what I consider to be his "so, there" look. "Feeling better?"

I stopped jiggling my legs and thought about it. "Yes. Much better."

## Chapter Thirty-Eight

### *Josephine*

When Norman said Mac had called to ask if he and Devi could stop by later, I didn't think anything of it. Last summer, they'd done that at least once a week, bringing the twins all bathed and ready for a cuddle.

When the doorbell rang, Norman answered. Not only had Devi and Mac come with the twins, but they'd brought Maddie, Lill, and Edna with them. Lill was wearing one of her fancy hats. She hardly steps out of the main building at Brookside without one these days. I even overheard another resident refer to her as the Hat Lady.

"This is lovely. I'm so glad you're all here. But . . . why are you all here?" They had the look of a delegation of sorts.

"We're here as witnesses," Devi said, sitting on the sofa and reaching out so Maddie could deposit Toby in her arms. Mac sat next to her, holding Lily.

When I stepped over to take one of the babies, Devi shook her head. That was peculiar, and it caused me to feel a stab of rejection.

"I'll be back in a minute," Maddie said, heading out the door.

To distract myself, I turned to Lill. "Another amazing hat."

"Yes, I can't imagine why I stopped wearing them." Lill patted the hat with an air of satisfaction.

I turned as the door closed behind Maddie to find her carrying a painting. She came and stood in front of me, biting her lip.

"Josephine, I want to present this to you, to thank you for all you've done for me and for Agatha and for Stanley. I apologize that I ever doubted your motives or questioned you or . . . Anyway, here."

She thrust the painting at me, and that's when I saw what it was.

"My dear girl. I don't know what to say."

"That may be a first," Mac said.

I'd looked up when he spoke, so I saw Devi poke him with her elbow. Deservedly.

Norman stepped up then and took the painting from me, and I gave Maddie a hug. I'm not much of a hugger, but I've found many more reasons to hug people since Lill, Devi, Mac, and Norman came into my life. And now Maddie. And Edna.

"That means she likes it," Devi said.

"It does." I leaned back and met Maddie's eyes. She'd shared with Devi and me her difficulties interpreting expressions and understanding social cues, so we tried to translate for her whenever we noticed her having a problem. "It's a marvelous painting. And I have the perfect spot for it." I pointed at the bare wall.

"And it just so happens, I have a hanger and a hammer handy," Norman said.

"You knew about this?"

"I did."

"Okay. I forgive you. I think."

"Shall we do that trial run?"

"Definitely."

In a couple of minutes, Norman, with all of us helping, had hammered the hanger into the correct spot. Then he ceremoniously hung the painting, and we all stared at it in silence. It was perfect.

"I'm so glad I kept that spot open," I told Maddie. "I had no idea why I felt I needed to do that. Until now."

"I like this one better than *Sea Watchers*," Lill said.

Devi turned to Maddie. "They really mean it. But even without words, you can see how much Josephine likes it."

"I do," I said, giving Maddie an intent look.

"So there's only one other small matter we need to take care of," Devi said. "It's high time we acknowledge Maddie's entry into the Josephine clan."

"Of course it isn't." I immediately realized how Maddie would interpret that. Literally, of course. "Because she's been a member for some time now. But I suppose this could be considered the official acknowledgment."

"I don't believe I ever got an official acknowledgment," Lill said. "So you should feel very special, Maddie."

"I'll drink to that." Norman walked into the room with a tray carrying both a pot of tea and a decanter of Scotch.

Maddie's head had turned back and forth as each of us spoke, and as I watched, I saw confusion replaced with delight. Smiling to myself, I poured tea while Norman poured Scotch. Then I led us in offering a toast.

"To Maddie, our newest family member. Welcome. We're so glad you're here." I paused, and we all lifted our cups and glasses. "Oh, and to Lill, who has been lacking a formal acknowledgment."

"What about me?" Devi said.

"And me," Mac added.

"And me?" Edna said, her voice a tentative squeak.

"To all of us, then," I said, making sure to salute both Edna and Maddie.

We clicked cups and glasses. Then Maddie stepped back, as if she still wasn't sure of her welcome.

I walked over to her, set my cup down, and looked her in the eye. "I hope you don't mind us adopting you? It means you must feel free to stop by whenever you want, to visit your painting. And us, of course."

There was a pause while Maddie obviously thought about that. Then she smiled. "I do. I mean, I will. Stop by, that is."

"I like this girl," I said, turning toward the others.

"Oh, so do we," Devi said.

## Chapter Thirty-Nine

### *Maddie*

My first family is a mystery. Lost before I could remember them. Then I discovered my second family wasn't who I thought they were, although I never doubted they loved me, and I loved them.

Now I have something I never imagined I could have. A third family. A wonderful mix of people who obviously care for each other, and who have now, amazingly, extended that caring to me.

What a strange and ultimately wonderful turn of events.

<<<>>>

# Author's Note

In the 1980s, I lived in Boston, and during that time I attended a reception at the Isabella Stewart Gardner Museum. The museum, formerly Gardner's home and designed by her to be an elegant frame for her extensive art collection, resembles a 15$^{th}$ century Venetian palace with a central courtyard.

When Gardner died of a heart attack in 1924, this home and its contents passed to a board of trustees with the proviso that the collection be maintained precisely as she had arranged it: nothing was to be added, removed, or moved, and any such change would give the board grounds to instantly dissolve the museum and transfer all its contents and property to "the President and Fellows of Harvard College" to dispose of as they saw fit.

What makes this museum particularly fascinating to me as an author is what happened there in the early hours of March 18, 1990. Shortly after midnight the museum guards admitted two men posing as police officers who claimed to be responding to a disturbance call. Once inside, the thieves tied up the guards and proceeded to loot the museum in a leisurely and seemingly random fashion. Thirteen works were removed including Rembrandt's *The Storm on the Sea of Galilee.*

Originally the total worth of the thieves' haul was estimated at two hundred million dollars, which made this the largest-value theft of private property ever recoded. This estimate was raised to five hundred million dollars in 2000, and some art dealers have suggested these works could now be worth as much as six hundred million dollars.

In the thirty years since the theft occurred, despite bizarre tips, false leads, possible underworld art sales, and secret communication through Boston's major newspapers, the identity of the robbers and the location of the artwork remain a mystery. The FBI believes the thieves were members of a criminal organization based in the mid-Atlantic region and New England. However, since the statute of limitations expired in 1995, the thieves and anyone who participated in the theft can no longer be prosecuted.

Given Gardner's will stipulated that nothing in her collection should be moved, the empty frames previously holding the stolen paintings remain hanging in their respective locations in the museum as placeholders for the artwork's potential return.

Since the museum had no insurance and was low on funds at the time of the robbery, the director solicited help from Sotheby's and Christie's auction houses to post a reward of one million dollars. This was increased to five million in 1997 and doubled to ten million in 2017, with an expiration date set for the end of the year.

To date, none of the art has been recovered.

This heist has provided inspiration to both television writers (*The Blacklist* and *The Simpsons*) and to other authors besides myself: *The Art Forger* (2012) by B.A. Shapiro and *Artful Deception* (2012) by James J. McGovern.

And, no, I had no idea that my visit to this museum nearly forty years ago would one day serve as an inspiration for me to write a novel. But once I introduced Norman Neuman, who spent his career recovering lost and stolen art, perhaps it was inevitable.

Sources for the factual information in this note include: The Isabella Stewart Gardner Museum, Wikipedia, Encyclopedia.com, and Factinate

If you enjoyed this book, I would be most appreciative if you would post a review on your favorite book site. Reviews help other readers decide whether to purchase the book, and they give me the credibility to advertise on book discovery sites.

# *About the Author*

The books Ann loved most as a child were those about horses. After reading Mary O'Hara's Wyoming ranch stories, she decided she would one day marry a rancher and own a racehorse, although not necessarily in that order.

Since it was clear to Ann, after reading My Friend Flicka and Green Grass of Wyoming, that money could be a sore point between ranchers and their wives, not to mention racehorses don't come cheap, she decided appropriate planning was needed. Thus she appended a "rich" to the rancher requirement.

But when she started dating, there were no ranchers in the offing, rich or otherwise. Instead, Ann fell in love with a fellow graduate student at the University of Kansas. Not only does her husband not share her love of horses, he doesn't even particularly like them, given that one stepped on him with deliberate intent when he was ten.

After years in academia, Ann took a turn down another road and began writing fiction. Her first novel, Dreams for Stones, was published on Christmas Day 2007, and has recently been re-released in electronic and print formats. The protagonist is both a university professor and part-time rancher—proof perhaps that dreams never truly go away, but continue to exert their influence in unexpected ways.

Those unexpected influences have continued to play a role in Ann's succeeding books, including this one.

# *Acknowledgments*

Although writing a novel requires solitude, no book gets published in isolation. Of the many people who have contributed to the process for this novel, I'm especially thankful to the following:

Delores Warner, who provided invaluable expertise to ensure the Graphoanalysis details in this series of novels are correct. Any errors in interpretation or description are mine. Thank you so much, Delores.

Pam Berehulke, who ensures that my grammar, punctuation, and timelines are perfect, although since I have a tendency to tinker, errors may have tiptoed their way in after Pam gave the book her imprimatur. If you should find an error in this novel, be assured I introduced it, not Pam.. Mea culpa, Pam.

Inspiration for the Babbling Brook series came, in part, from my experiences as a member of the Circle Singers, a community chorus. Singing with the chorus at local retirement communities in the Cincinnati area provided me with details that I've used in this series.

I also want to acknowledge the tremendous contributions of the members of the Women's Fiction Critique Group on Facebook who were my first readers: Gail Cleare, Margaret Johnson, Karin Davies, Bella Ellwood-Clayton, Linda Chalk, Sarah Hawthorn, Caitlin Avery, Diane Byington, Enni Tuomisalo, and Diana L. Patz McDowell. Special thanks to Andrea Barton for her detailed comments and to Mikhail Rapoport, the winner of a character-naming contest, who provided me with the perfect name: Mekyle.

And to all those who have written to comment on my stories, especially those of you who have told me my novels have been a source of comfort or distraction during tough times, thank you!

My gratitude as well to everyone who has posted a review of one of my books. Your kindness makes it easier for others to discover my novels.

And above all, thanks to my husband, who lights up my life and makes it possible for me to be a full-time writer.

# Also by Ann Warner

## Dreams for Stones
## Book One of the Dreams Trilogy

Available as a free download in multiple formats
Indie Next Generation Book Award Finalist
Audio and Print editions available

A man holding fast to grief and a woman who lets go of love too easily. It will take all the magic of old diaries and a children's story to heal these two. Caught in grief and guilt over his wife's death, English professor Alan Francini is determined never to feel that much pain again. He avoids new relationships and keeps even his best friend at arms' length. His major solace is his family's ranch south of Denver.

Children's book editor Kathy Jamison has learned through a lifetime of separations and a broken engagement that letting go is easier than hanging on. Then she meets Alan, and for once, begins to believe a lasting relationship is possible. But Alan panics and pushes her away into the arms of his best friend. Now the emotions of three people are at stake as they struggle to find a way to transform their broken dreams into a foundation for a more hopeful future.

## Persistence of Dreams
## Book Two of the Dreams Trilogy

Audio, Electronic, and Print editions available

Lost memories and surprising twists of mystery. Alan, Kathy, and Charles's story continues. The ending of his love affair with Kathy and an arsonist seeking revenge are the catalysts that alter the shape and direction of Charles's life. Forced to find both a new place to live and a way to ease his heartache,

Charles finds much more as he reaches out to help his neighbor Luz Montalvo. Helping Luz forces Charles to come to grips with his fractured friendships and the fragmented memories of his childhood.

Luz Montalvo was a carefree college student until her parents died in a car crash. Frantic not to lose her younger siblings to foster care, Luz took them on the run. After nearly a year scraping by as an apartment manager, she's just beginning to feel safe when she discovers her newest tenant is her worst nightmare, a deputy district attorney.

## *Unexpected Dreams*
## *Book Three in the Dreams Trilogy*

### Electronic Editions Available

Murder made to look like an accident, family secrets, interfering mothers, lovers in conflict. All combine in a satisfying mix in this contemporary romantic mystery.

Phoebe Whitney-Tolliver has just ended a long-term relationship and begun a new position as the Chief Accident Investigator for the City and County of Denver. She has also fulfilled a lifelong dream—that of owning a horse. These changes bring Phoebe into contact with horse owner and attorney Sam Talbot and Luz and Charles Larimore.

Phoebe helps Charles, a district attorney, and Luz, his wife, in determining whether a traffic accident was actually murder, while Sam locates information about Luz's Chilean family. Eventually the four of them come up against Luz's murderous uncle, a man determined to maintain control of the family's large estancia in Chile. The uncle is a formidable foe, one who will require all the wiles and skill Phoebe, Sam, Charles, and Luz possess to overcome.

# *Doubtful*

Endorsed by Compulsion Reads

Red Ribbon Award - Wishing Shelf Independent Book Awards

Electronic Edition Available

Doubtful Sound, New Zealand: For Dr. Van Peters, Doubtful is a retreat after a false accusation all but ends her scientific career. For David Christianson, Doubtful is a place of respite after a personal tragedy is followed by an unwelcome notoriety.

Neither is looking for love or even friendship. Each wants only to make it through another day. But when violence comes to Doubtful, Van and David's only chance of survival will be each other.

# *Absence of Grace*

Available as a free download in multiple formats

The memory of an act committed when she was nineteen weaves a dark thread through Clen McClendon's life. It is a darkness Clen ignores until the discovery of her husband's infidelity propels her on a quest for her own redemption and forgiveness. At first, her journeying provides few answers and peace remains elusive. Then Clen makes a decision that is both desperate and random to go to Wrangell, Alaska. There she will meet Gerrum Kirsey and learn that choices are never truly random, and they always have consequences.

## *Counterpointe*

### Endorsed by Compulsion Reads
### Electronic Edition Available

Art, science, love, and ambition collide as a dancer on the verge of achieving her dreams is badly injured. Afterward, Clare Eliason rushes into a marriage with Rob Chapin. The marriage falters, propelling Clare and Rob on journeys of self-discovery. Rob joins a scientific expedition to Peru, where he discovers how easy it is to die. Clare's journey, which takes her only a few blocks from the Boston apartment she shared with Rob, is no less profound. During their time apart, each will have a chance to save a life. One will succeed, one will not. Finally, they will face the most difficult quest of all, navigating the space that lies between them.

## *Love and Other Acts of Courage*

### Wishing Shelf Independent Book Awards Finalist
### Electronic Edition Available

A freighter collides with a yacht and abandons the survivors. A couple is left behind by a dive boat.

These are the dramatic events that force changes in maritime attorney Max Gildea's carefully organized life, where, win, lose, or settle out of court, he gets paid and paid handsomely. As he represents the only survivor of the yacht sinking and gets involved in the search for the couple missing from a dive trip, his reawakening emotions catapult him into the chaos of sorrow and joy that are the necessary ingredients of a life lived fully.

## *Memory Lessons*
### Electronic Edition Available

Glenna Girard has passed through the agony and utter darkness of an unimaginable loss. It is only in planning her escape, from her marriage and her current circumstances, that she manages to start moving again, toward a place where she can live in anonymity and atone for the unforgivable mistake she has made.

As she takes tentative steps into the new life she is so carefully shaping, she has no desire to connect with other people. But fate has other ideas, bringing her a family who can benefit from her help if only she will give it. And a man, Jack Ralston, who is everything she needs to live fully again, if Glenna will just let herself see it.

## *Vocabulary of Light*
### Electronic Edition Available

Living in Puerto Rico might sound like a dream to some people, but for Maggie Chase it's more of a challenge than she's looking for. Maggie, who has a PhD in biochemistry, agreed to put her husband's career first after the birth of their daughters, and that has now led to Mike accepting the position of CEO of the Lillith Pharmaceuticals plant in San Juan. Struggling to fit into the bilingual, Latin culture of Puerto Rico in the late 1980s, Maggie's adjustment is aided by the friendships she develops. Friendships that bring both dark and light into her life, and eventually demand of her an inner strength and resilience she didn't know she was capable of.

Made in the USA
Middletown, DE
27 July 2020